"I'd like very much to talk to you about your sister."

Dominic's voice was smooth as he went on to ask, "Will you have lunch with me today?"

"Under the circumstances," Honor said acidly, "I think not."

"You're very sure of yourself," he said softly, moving over to where Honor sat. "Very confident and very hostile, too. But when you looked at me in that boardroom earlier today, I saw something in your eyes that no woman would have allowed to show—if she hadn't meant it."

Suddenly Honor's heart seemed to flip right over as Dominic reached out to touch her face. She was utterly lost for words and, for an aching second, submitted to his caress.

"I wasn't wrong," he said softly. "You may think you hate me, Honor, but if you imagine I intend to give you up without a struggle, you're very much mistaken."

MADELEINE KER is a self-described "compulsive writer." In fact, Madeleine has been known to deliver six romances in less than a year. The author is married, and in addition to a writing career, she is a graduate student at Durham University.

Books by Madeleine Ker

HARLEQUIN PRESENTS

739—WORKING RELATIONSHIP
778—OUT OF THIS DARKNESS
795—FIRE OF THE GODS
884—DANGER ZONE
947—IMPACT
1090—FRAZER'S LAW
1114—THE WILDER SHORES OF LOVE

HARLEQUIN ROMANCE

2595—VOYAGE OF THE MISTRAL
2636—THE STREET OF THE FOUNTAIN
2709—ICE PRINCESS
2716—HOSTAGE

MADELEINE KER

judgement

Harlequin Books

TORONTO • NEW YORK • LONDON
AMSTERDAM • PARIS • SYDNEY • HAMBURG
STOCKHOLM • ATHENS • TOKYO • MILAN

Harlequin Presents first edition January 1989
ISBN 0-373-11138-X

Original hardcover edition published in 1987
by Mills & Boon Limited

Printed in U.S.A.

CHAPTER ONE

'THEIR Imperial Majesties Blair-Winship have finished their earth-shaking report.' Mike Wetherall shrugged on his maroon leather jacket, and held the office door open for Honor. 'It's been on the Director's desk since lunch time.'

Honor's expression didn't brighten at the news. 'Has he read it, then?'

'Yep.'

'And?'

'Panic stations. Major staff meeting for Tuesday next week. We're all getting memos about it in the morning. You know the old ComTech rule? When in trouble or in doubt, wave your arms and scream and shout.'

Honor smiled as they walked down the stairs. 'You're well informed.'

'As always, boss, as always.'

She got on well with Mike Wetherall. Like Honor herself, he had worked for ComTech almost since its inception four years ago—when the future of Communication Technology, to give the company its proper title, had been somewhat brighter than it was today. When she'd been put in charge of the department last year, his congratulations had been genuine.

They walked from the big Cromwell Centre to Victoria Station, as they usually did at the end of each working day. 'I take it the news is generally bad?' she enquired.

'From what I hear, Blair-Winship confirm that the LP-550 is turning into a financial disaster.'

'Oh, damn . . .'

'Pointless exercise, if you ask me,' Mike added drily. 'The

analysts have just earned themselves several thousand quid for telling Mark what you or I could have told him for free. The real point is what he's going to do about it.'

Mike Wetherall was right. The first signs of the setback had been picked up in their own division. And most people knew the reason. The LP-550 had been a brilliant product, containing some very highly advanced technology; but within weeks of its launch last autumn, two microprocessors of almost identical design had been brought out by relative newcomers to the scene. The profits which ComTech had been relying on so hopefully had been reduced by almost two-thirds . . .

Honor bought an evening paper at a kiosk, and in an atmosphere of slight gloom they walked down the stairs to wait for their trains; his to East Putney, where he lived with his wife and two children, hers to the opposite direction, to Highbury.

'Are you meeting Pru tonight?' Mike asked, glancing around hopefully for Honor's younger sister among the crowds.

'She's got the afternoon off, for some reason.'

'Oh.' Mike looked disappointed. People always looked disappointed when Pru didn't turn up; she was that sort of girl. 'A special dispensation from her future father-in-law?'

'I suppose so,' Honor nodded.

'I imagine she can hardly sleep for excitement these days?'

'She seems to take everything in her stride.' Honor smiled. 'One of the benefits of being nineteen, maybe. But she's very happy.'

'So she should be,' Mike said feelingly, 'marrying her boss's only son and heir. When young Mog Lambert inherits Lambert Exports, he's going to be disgustingly rich. Pru's done very well for herself.' He ran a hand wearily through his close-cropped fair hair, then adjusted his horn-rimmed spectacles. 'I'll tell you one thing this LP-550 business brings home, Honor. Computing moves too damned quickly. I'm thirty-two, and I'm worn out.'

'Oh, come on,' she protested.

'The pay isn't good enough to make up for the loss of my youth and beauty. This is your first job. I've already seen two computer firms go down.'

Honor looked at him quickly. 'You think ComTech is going down, too?' she asked anxiously. 'Just because of the LP-550?'

'Let's face it,' he grimaced, 'it's dog eat dog in this business. Mark may be a gifted designer, but he's not a businessman. He's too impulsive. He takes risks. If he isn't careful, one of the big outfits from the smoke will swallow ComTech up one of these days, and then we'll all be out of a job.'

The buffet of hot air signalled the imminent arrival of Mike's train, and with a wave, he hurried off down the escalator. Honor walked glumly to the opposite platform, reaching it just as her own train pulled in.

Rattling on the underground, Honor's thoughts were preoccupied with what Mike Wetherall had said. The LP-550 had been a hugely expensive venture for a relatively small firm. Communications Technology had enjoyed a meteoric success in the home computers field, thanks to Mark MacDonald's innovative brilliance. But perhaps Mark had gone just that bit too far this time? Tuesday might tell, but it was scarcely a happy prospect to look forward to.

She turned her mind to Prudence's wedding instead. There wasn't much she could do about ComTech, whereas her younger sister's welfare had always been her direct concern ever since she'd been fourteen, when their mother had died.

On the face of it, the match was a dazzling one for Pru.

Mog Lambert was a handsome young man with immense prospects, and he was obviously mad about Pru. He was the son of Morgan Lambert Senior, the Chairman of Lambert Exports, where Pru had been working for less than a year, and one day he was going to inherit the company. And that would effectively make Pru very rich.

But Pru was barely nineteen, and though she was sparklingly intelligent, and equipped with a beautiful, adult body, she was also not yet a mature woman. It had more than once occurred to Honor that her younger sister might be rushing into marriage too recklessly.

Yet as she thought about Pru, she couldn't stop the affectionate smile from creeping across her mouth. She had a very soft spot for Prudence. Unlike their elder brother Toby, Pru had inherited none of their father's darker spirit—and all of their mother's joy for life. She was gay, vulnerable and sweet-natured, a girl who loved to tease and flirt, to dress in pretty clothes, to dance and sing. Pru was going to get her own way, as she always did.

The flat she and Prudence shared was half a mile from the tube station, and Honor's heart always lifted on the fifteen-minute walk. Their street's residents were among the most dedicated gardeners in London, and each little front garden was ablaze with peony roses and red-hot pokers, lupins and delphiniums. The flat itself had a tiny plot, but she and Pru had filled the garden with flowers, and it matched anything else the street had to show.

She walked up the garden path, sniffing the welcoming scent of the honeysuckle, and pushed through the door.

'Pru!' she called. 'Anyone home?'

But when Pru came slowly out of her bedroom, Honor's heart jumped in shock at her sister's appearance. Prudence O'Hara's face was pale and drawn, and her eyes were red with crying. She tried to smile, but her lips quivered with the effort.

'Pru?' Honor reached out instinctively. 'What is it, baby?'

'Oh . . . nothing much.' Pru slumped down, and looked up at Honor with haunted eyes, all her prettiness marred. 'I'm just not getting married to Mog any more. That's all.'

'What's happened?' Honor sat beside her sister anxiously. 'Have you and Mog quarrelled?'

'I haven't seen Mog.' Pru fought to hold back the tears. 'Mog's in—in America.'

'America?' Honor echoed in disbelief. 'What on earth is he doing in America?'

'His father sent him there. Mr Lambert says the wedding's off. Because of D-daddy and Toby.' This time the tears welled up regardless, and Pru covered her eyes with shaky fingers. 'Oh, Honor! It's s-so awful.'

Honor put her arms round her sister's shoulders, and drew her close. She already had a good idea what had happened today, and her normally gentle mouth was set in a very angry line. But as Pru sobbed, she kept her voice tender.

'Tell me what happened, Pru. Everything.'

'He just called me into his office this morning,' Pru said unsteadily, wiping her cheeks with her wrists. 'As I was leaving. He said certain facts had come to his notice, and he couldn't allow the wedding to go ahead.'

'Facts about your family?' Honor asked quietly.

Pru nodded. 'Th-then he said that Mog was going to be working in America for a long time, and that I m-mustn't hope to see him again. And he said it would be better if I resigned from Lambert's. And . . .'

'You've lost your job!'

'He's going to g-give me a year's pay, and get me another job, but oh . . .'

'Oh, Pru,' Honor said gently, stroking the auburn hair away from Prudence's cheeks. 'Why didn't you ring me at

ComTech? I'd have come home at once.'

'I didn't want you to.' Pru held Honor's hand in both her own, and her tear-filled eyes were large and tragic. 'But I'm so glad you're back now.'

'Mog knew about Toby and Daddy,' Honor said. 'Didn't he?'

'Yes. But he'd never told his father. I pleaded with him to, but he always said there was time enough to bring it up later. Pru, it's horrible. I found out—he had us investigated by a private detective.'

'Mr Lambert? I don't believe it!'

'Look.' Pru picked something off the floor, and gave it to Honor. It was a red manilla folder, with the word *Confidential* stamped across it in black letters. Honor flipped it open. It was a shock to see the sheaf of photographs pinned to the typewritten report inside. High-resolution black and white prints. Telephoto lens stuff.

One of her father, an old passport picture blown up. One of Toby, walking out of a doorway, thin shoulders hunched against a drizzle of rain, his expression sour. That had been taken, she knew, outside his flat in Earl's Court.

And one of herself, leaving the ComTech office, dark hair fanned out by the wind.

'Where did you get this?' she asked Pru sharply.

'It was on his desk,' Pru said dully. 'He was looking at it while he talked to me.'

'You took it off his desk?'

'I just had to know.' Pru sighed shakily. 'I couldn't believe what had happened. So I waited until he went out for lunch, and then I went into his office, and took it out of his drawer.'

'That wasn't very wise,' Honor said quietly, but inwardly reflected that she might have done the same. She glanced at the heading on the notepaper. A neat logo of a black bird. *Raven Security, London.* God! How long had some anonymous, mackintoshed figure been spying on all of them, unobserved and unsuspected?

Honor read the typed report with a hard ball of anger in her chest.

It was all there, in neutral, terse prose. The gradual disintegration of her father's career since their mother's death. His drinking, his visits to Rosslands for treatment for alcoholism, even the details of his minor criminal record. And a final, dismissive sentence: 'The evidence points inevitably to the conclusion that Patrick O'Hara died an alcoholic.'

It looked so ugly, there in black and white.

The bare facts of Toby's life looked similarly cruel. Unemployment, theft, drugs, petty fraud. A failure, the son of a failure, heading for the same wretched conclusion. Poor Toby, poor, weak victim of his own irresponsibility . . .

What coldly unfeeling mind had compiled all this information? she wondered. She felt nausea rise in her throat as she flicked through the pages, and understood what Pru had gone through this afternoon.

At twenty-five, Honor was past feeling shame or humiliation over her father's tragedy or her brother's weakness. Pain, yes, she was used to that; but she'd always had to accept that her life was her own responsibility—just as Daddy's life had been his responsibility, and Toby's life was his. She'd done all she could for Dad, God knew; but there was a point beyond which you could do nothing. And at that point you had to accept that other people's mistakes just weren't your fault—accept that, or let your own life be ruined . . .

But Pru, sweet, vulnerable Pru, was too young to have achieved that balance. This, coming on top of Morgan Lambert's bombshell, would have cut into her young nerves like a knife . . .

The next section dealt with Honor herself. 'The evidence is that Honor O'Hara forms the central link for her family. She is an unusually competent person, who habitually intervened with money or assistance to keep her father out of serious trouble, while he was alive. The same appears to be true of her brother since then. She also appears to act as a surrogate mother for her younger sister.'

She is an unusually competent person. The patronising phrase stuck in her craw almost more than anything else she'd read. The personal details that followed were accurate. Little had been omitted, not even her salary and details of her mortgage. How on earth had they found out that sort of thing? There was a summary at the end, referring to Pru.

'Prudence O'Hara appears to be of good character'. She let her eyes run down the rather non-committal paragraph. 'There is no evidence of narcotics or alcohol abuse. She has no criminal record. Morgan Lambert II is her only regular male contact, though it is known she has been involved with other men before her employment at Lambert Exports.'

The flare of anger almost made Honor rip the beautifully typed sheets in two. How *dared* they? How *dared* anyone pry into their life, their past, their family, like this? It was obscene. Damn that old man. And damn his spy. Teeth gritted, Honor shuffled the report back into order.

She was grateful, at least, for the anger that kept the tears at bay. She needed to be strong and comforting for Prudence's sake right now.

'I'm sorry,' she said quietly. 'So sorry, piglet. This might all work out in time——'

'It won't.' Pru twisted her hands together. 'He said that given our family situation the idea of marriage was quite impossible. He said he could forgive Morgan choosing a wife of no fortune and no family, but it w-wasn't simply that. Morgan would inherit Lambert Enterprises one day.

He'd move in the highest social circles, and I must surely see that a wife whose father had been an alcoholic, and whose brother was a—a petty thief and a drug addict, could only be a disaster for him.'

The blind, cruel arrogance almost took Honor's breath away. 'What did you say?' she asked tightly.

'That I could never do anything to harm Mog.' Pru's voice sounded distant, as though someone else was speaking the words for her. 'That if Mog didn't want to marry me any more, that was it as far as I was concerned.' She raised bruised-looking eyes to Honor's face. 'Toby's not really a drug addict, is he?'

'No.' Honor smiled. 'And Daddy wasn't quite an alcoholic, either. But people aren't always kind about the weaknesses of others, you know that.'

'Yes.'

'When did Mog leave for America?'

'I don't know,' Pru said, rubbing her face. 'It must have been some time since Sunday night.'

'And you haven't heard a word from him about any of this?'

'Nothing.' She looked away. 'His father said it was Mog's own decision to go to America.'

'With no message for you?' Honor asked with dry disbelief.

'I think he'd threatened to disinherit Mog. I don't think Mog had any choice.'

'Ah.' That explained a great many things. Disinheritance was an unpleasant threat—they'd all heard it from their own father at one time or another. Except that in Morgan Lambert's case it meant a great deal more.

'There's a letter, as well,' Prudence told her dully. 'At the back.'

Honor found it. It was addressed to Morgan Lambert Senior, and like the report, it had been typewritten. It was brief and very much to the point.

Dear Morgan,

I am enclosing the report you asked for. I think you'll agree that aspects of Prudence O'Hara's family circumstances are, as you suspected, unfortunate.

You also asked me to give a personal opinion of the young lady's suitability as a wife for your son. My meetings with her have been brief, but in my judgement the marriage would be extremely unwise.

We can discuss this topic further, any time you wish.

It was signed, in black ink, *Dominic Raven.*

Honor closed the folder, and noted absently that her fingers were shaking.

'Who is Dominic Raven?' she asked in a dry voice.

'He runs a big security agency,' Pru said, leaning back in the sofa, and staring listlessly ahead. 'God, I've got such a headache.' Honor recognised the signs of emotional exhaustion, and mentally explored the contents of the medicine chest in the bathroom. 'Dominic's a friend of the family,' Pru went on tiredly. 'Of Mog's family. They all talk about him as though he were some kind of oracle. I met him once or twice. He's big and dark and a bit awe-inspiring, but I thought he was lovely.'

'It seems the feeling wasn't mutual.' Honor fetched two aspirins and a glass of water from the bathroom, and waited while Pru obediently took them.

Mog, she thought absently, was probably as much a victim of this whole sorry business as Prudence herself. He was very young, only three years older than Pru, and very much in his father's power. Morgan Lambert Senior was a formidable man, quite capable of carrying out his threat to leave Mog effectively destitute. Mog would have had very little choice but to obey.

Yet she found it hard to forgive Mog for not having attempted to tell Pru himself. He must have known how painful it would be for her to face the old man alone, with no warning or explanation. Maybe, though, he hadn't had any choice about that, either.

But he was safely in America now. And Pru was going to have to face the mortification of a public rejection, the lingering embarrassment of being a target for every malicious, pointing finger. That was intolerable.

'Honor.' Pru touched her hand gently. 'Don't look like that,' she pleaded. 'I always felt in my bones that something like this was going to happen. It was too good to be true.'

'Oh, Pru . . .'

'Promise me one thing. Promise me you won't try and do anything!'

Honor shook her head. 'You don't seem to understand how you've been insulted. We've got to see Mr Vaughan about this.'

'Oh no, no! Solicitors never helped anything.' Pru gave her a twisted smile. 'And breach-of-promise suits are a bit out of fashion, aren't they?'

'Justice is never out of fashion,' Honor said grimly. 'We *must* see Mr Vaughan, Pru.'

'No!' Pru whimpered, obviously upset by the idea.

'To withdraw an offer of marriage without good reason is a very serious thing.' Honor stroked Pru's trembling hand. 'What possible right does this man Raven have to go around advising Mog's family that you aren't suitable?'

'He's a sort of family advisor. They trust him.'

'But this amounts to slander,' Honor said, pointing at the

file. 'It's important for your sake tha you clear your name, little one.'

Pru shook her head. 'No,' she repeated. 'It's you who don't understand. Toby and Daddy *are* a good reason. That's the whole point. I couldn't bear to have all our family history bandied around in some courtroom.' She gestured at the file. 'What's happened already is enough, isn't it? Besides . . .' Pru's eyes were pathetic. 'Mog doesn't want me any more. Mr Vaughan won't change that, will he?'

'I think you should wait to hear from Mog before you decide whether he wants you or not,' Honor said gently. 'He'll write soon, I'm sure of it.'

'He won't!'

There wasn't much she could say to that. 'Is Mr Lambert going to make any kind of announcement?' Honor asked thoughtfully.

'He doesn't want any talk,' Pru said tiredly. 'If people ask me, I have to say we've both changed our minds. He just wants the whole thing to blow over quietly . . .'

'Like a cold,' Honor said grimly.

'Don't say anything to Mr Lambert,' Pru pleaded. 'I can tell you feel like going and telling him he's been wrong. Please don't! It'll only make things much worse!'

Pru was getting more agitated by the minute, and Honor soothed her as best she could. 'I won't do *anything* you don't want me to,' she nodded. 'You need a rest now,' she went on softly. 'Why not lie down, and I'll bring you a cup of tea in a moment.'

'Not until you promise,' Pru pleaded. Her face showed her exhaustion quite clearly. 'I know you'll want to go and do something to help me. I'm begging you to just let it be.'

'I promise,' Honor said. 'Now go and lie down, and I'll come and talk to you in a minute.'

Pru nodded, and stood up like a sleepwalker.

'I want to forget the whole thing,' she said dully. 'Just for the next few hours, I want to pretend it hasn't happened.'

Making the tea, Honor felt a wave of mingled pity, sadness and anger wash over her. Poor little Pru! If anyone deserved happiness, she did. When she'd met Mog, it had seemed that for once in her life, fate had dealt a decent hand. Love had been within reach. Love, marriage, a family of her own—all the things that Pru had missed in her own short life, and that would seem all the more precious to her.

She'd failed Pru. Failed to foresee the danger that should have been so obvious. God, she'd been so blind! Little Pru was an innocent, but she herself ought to have known better. It ought to have registered, a long time ago. Rich young men didn't marry poor young women. Not in real life. Not when their family circumstances were—what was the word Mr Raven had used? *Unfortunate.* Society's darlings didn't marry *unfortunate* ladies.

When she went into Pru's bedroom with the tea, Pru was already asleep. Her face looked unbelievably childlike and vulnerable, and there were tear stains on her cheeks. Honor stood for a moment, watching her sister sleep, the way she'd done so many times over the past ten years. Just how was she going to comfort Pru this time? There wasn't an answer.

Honor had never missed her mother as much as she did right now. Sometimes it was so hard not to have someone to talk to. You couldn't have told your problems to Dad; he had been too crippled by alcohol and self-pity to give a damn about anything beyond his own feelings. But until he'd died of a heart attack two years ago, he had at least been her only surviving parent.

Anyway, it was probably just as well that Dad wasn't alive today to see the legacy of his drinking . . .

And Toby—Toby was too young, for all that he was a

year her senior. He would only have reacted with a pathetic explosion of meaningless family pride.

She tiptoed out, and went into the garden. The summer sky was a deep, lovely blue. She wandered along the crumbling garden wall, absently pulling a few weeds from between the rock-plants she and Pru had planted in the crevices in the stones.

Damn the social vanity of men like Morgan Lambert and Dominic Raven! Damn people who treated other humans like pawns on a chessboard! What monstrous egotism would make anyone come between two young people in love? And why *should* Pru have to give up her job, just to smooth the path of a rich old man's will? She'd met Morgan Lambert Senior several times since Mog had announced his intention of marrying Pru, and she'd never liked his thin smile or his cold eyes.

Her face creased in anger and sadness. Where her sister was vivacious, Honor's beauty was tranquil. And though she didn't have Prudence's gaiety, there was a calmness, a poise about her, that was somehow very striking. Her movements were graceful, feminine, and either she had faultless taste, or there was some special quality in her figure, because everything she wore seemed to sit perfectly on her soft lines.

Her colouring, too, was striking, a combination of jet-black hair and green eyes, together with clear, flawless skin. A nose that was neat without snubness, a mouth that was full, drawn as exquisitely as if by some great painter, and the fine bones of her cheeks, temples and chin, ensured that she would remain beautiful long after the age when most women had ceased to have any interest for men.

Yet there was also a touch-me-not quality about Honor, very different from Pru's warm allure, that had infuriated more than one man in the past. And she was articulate enough to have been able to bring some colour to Morgan

Lambert's cheeks, had Pru not bound her to silence. No, she wouldn't go stalking off to confront the old man, the way her instincts urged her to. But if she ever met Mr Morgan Lambert, or Mr Dominic Raven, she swore she would not restrain her tongue!

Pru's done very well for herself. Mike's words came back to her, coloured with irony. Well, Pru was in for a public humiliation that was going to be very hard for her. She'd reflected earlier today that Pru's love for Mog might have been just that little bit shallow; if so, that would be an advantage right now.

And damn Toby and Daddy for their irresponsibility in the first place! It was hard not to feel that some blame attached to them. Harder still to accept that there was no way they could fight back. But Pru was probably right; nothing would be served by dragging the whole sorry business through a blaze of publicity. It would only mean more pain and more mortification.

She turned and glanced at Pru's bedroom window. The pretty chintz fabric was fluttering in the evening breeze.

Poor litle Pru, she thought sadly. Is there anyone lately who hasn't let you down?

The boardroom was crowded on Tuesday, and Honor had to share a corner with Mike Wetherall and a lethally barbed cactus, which snagged her elegant black suit as she brushed past it.

'This,' Mike remarked out of the corner of his mouth, 'has all the hallmarks of a wake.'

'Hmmm,' Honor said, examining the tear in her skirt.

Apart from the office staff, the boffins were there too, computer engineers from the ComTech factory in Kent, who seldom commuted to London. Honor also recognised Mr Peartree, the factory manager. A real gathering of the clan.

None of them looked very cheerful.

'Look at their expressions,' Mike went on unsympathetically. 'Sufferance is the badge of all our tribe. And that goes for you too, boss. You look tired.'

'Hmmm,' Honor said again. She'd had a bad few days with Pru. She had rather hoped that the resilience of being nineteen, combined with Pru's natural bounce, would have ensured a speedy recovery. But Pru had been even more distraught than she'd at first realised. There had been nothing shallow about her love for Mog Lambert.

Given Pru's low emotional state, it was hardly surprising that she'd also gone down with a cold. She couldn't have gone back to Lambert's, of course, after what had happened, and she'd sent in her resignation. Losing her job, as well as her fiancé, had meant her moping at home all day; and that had scarcely helped. Nor had Mog so much as dropped her a note. Maybe he, like Pru, had been spending his past few days starting countless letters, only to tear each one up.

'I wonder whether our revered leader has something up his sleeve for today,' Mike speculated, oblivious to her silence. 'He'd better have, or things are going to get very tight round here.'

Honor sighed, dragging her thoughts away from Pru. It was so selfish to dwell on her own problems when the firm might be teetering towards financial disaster.

'I don't believe things are all that bad,' she said firmly. She hadn't said anything to Mike about Pru yet. As far as he knew, she was at home with a bad cold, but sooner or later she was going to have to agree some kind of story with Pru, and release it for general circulation. 'We'll all just have to tighten our belts, that's all.'

'Aye, aye,' Mike murmured, glancing over her shoulder. 'The bank haven't called in the Receiver, have they?'

She looked round quickly. Mark MacDonald, the man

who had singlehandedly founded ComTech, was coming into the boardroom, accompanied by two other men. One was the firm's chief accountant, Ian Thompson, a dry sixty-year-old with a wealth of experience in the City; and the other was a stranger to Honor.

Dark-haired, dark-eyed, and very tall, he looked around Mark's age—say thirty-six. Quite unlike Mark, who was almost painfully shy and diffident, this man also had an unmistakable aura of authority; it was there in every move he made.

'Is he from the Receiver?' she whispered to Mike.

'I don't know who he is,' Mike shrugged. 'He looks like trouble, though.'

The stranger fascinated her for some reason, drawing her attention irresistibly. She knew she'd never seen him before, yet his presence was so striking that Honor was aware of a kind of inner recognition. She only had time to take in a strongly made, tanned face, marked by very black eyebrows and eyelashes; a mouth that could be either cruel or devastatingly sexual; and an utter lack of weakness or gentleness.

He sat down beside Mark, his obsidian-black eyes drifting casually across the crowded room. She wanted to look away before his eyes met hers, but somehow she couldn't. The dark gaze met her own, and as it did so Honor suddenly felt the full force of an alien personality. Magnetic, male, dominant. Unaccountably, her cheeks flushed scarlet as the blood rushed to her face.

That he had noted her idiotic blush was clear by the sardonic tilt of one enquiring eyebrow.

She bit her lip furiously as she looked down, and sank further into her chair. Damn! What was she behaving like a schoolgirl for? She hadn't lost her poise like this since she was a teenager.

She couldn't help looking up again, and when she did so,

those dark, male eyes were still on her. Honor sensed, rather than actually saw, the amusement and curiosity that were registering in the saturnine face. *Damn!* This time she stared boldly back, determined not to be outfaced. For a few seconds their eyes were locked, her whole body hot and cold by turns with the effort of not looking away.

There was a sudden glitter, not actually a smile, in his eyes; and then he was lowering his head to listen to something Mark MacDonald was saying to him. She almost gasped in relief, as though iron fingers had released their grip on her heart.

'Well, well, well.' Mike Wetherall was watching with considerable interest from behind his horn-rims. 'I take it you two have met somewhere before, after all?'

'I've never seen him in my life,' she retorted briefly, her skin still tingling.

'*He* doesn't seem to think so,' Mike grinned. 'He's a good-looking son of a gun. And what with you looking all romantic and interesting in that black dress——' He lowered his glasses to inspect Honor's blush more closely. 'My love is like a red, red rose.'

Mark MacDonald rapped the table sharply at that point, and cleared his throat. 'Right. I'm sorry to drag you all away from your busy schedules, but this needn't take long at all.'

Honor studiously avoided looking at anyone at all, staring determinedly down at her hands. Yet as Mark started talking, she had the hot conviction that those black eyes were still watching her.

There was nothing unexpected in Mark's opening sentences. As she'd anticipated, he started with the launch of the LP-550 last year. An indifferent name for a product, she thought absently; it didn't trip off the tongue easily. She listened as he quoted the disastrous sales figures, and the even worse projections made by Blair-Winship.

'The LP-550 was not only a highly advanced home computer,' Mark was saying, 'but, as you all know, was marketed at an unprecedently reasonable price. It should have brought in substantial profits.

'The Blair-Winship report pinpoints the failure to the launch of two rival microprocessors at around the same time last autumn. OK, we all know that by now. These machines bore remarkable similarities to the ComTech product, both in intrinsic design, and in packaging and price.' He spoke, as always, in a quiet monotone, punctuated with occasional trendy words like *OK* and *right*. Not the world's greatest public speaker.

Unable to bear the feeling that she was being watched any longer, Honor summoned the courage to lift her eyes cautiously. But the stranger wasn't looking at her after all. He, too, was looking steadily down, appearing to listen intently. What sort of voice would he have? Deep, harsh, but cultured, she guessed. No OKs or rights. Why had his stare upset her so much?

'... and their report expresses some doubts whether, given the unique quality of the research which the company put into the LP-550, such a carefully timed launch by our competitors could be entirely coincidental. OK? They feel that an accidental or deliberate transmission of confidential material may have been involved.'

There was a pause. Honor felt Mike Wetherall stiffen beside her just as realisation dawned in her own mind. Had she understood Mark's convoluted sentences right? Expressions of doubt were reflected in other faces, too, as Mark went on in the same quiet way.

'Therefore, I have taken the advice of both Blair-Winship and Mr Thomspon in commissioning a second report on the possibility I've just mentioned.' For the first time he looked up, and Honor could see weariness in the Director's face. 'This is not to be regarded as in the nature of a witch-hunt, or anything of that sort. It is purely an attempt to improve security within ComTech. That is why I have called this meeting.'

Oh, good God! Honor glanced at Mike, who was looking as uncomfortable as she felt. Industrial espionage? Someone selling ComTech's secrets to the opposition? The idea was crazy, melodramatic.

Mark inclined his head towards the man beside him. 'This is Dominic Raven.'

The dark stranger nodded slightly to the room as Mark made the introduction.

Honor felt shock numb her. As if in a dream, she heard Mark go on, 'Mr Raven will be personally in charge of the enquiry, and over the next couple of weeks he may wish to interview some of you. It must be clear that no personal slight will be implied.' He cleared his throat. 'I'm asking for the co-operation of each and every one of you in this. I want you to give him every facility. The future of Communication Technology may well depend on the advice Mr Raven can give us.'

CHAPTER TWO

'So *that's* who he is,' Mike whispered. 'The Raven himself! The Prince of Darkness is a gentleman, by the looks of him.'

Honor, too, was staring across the room at him, grains of ice forming in her blood. *Dominic Raven.*

If he was aware that Honor's eyes—and every other eye in the room—were riveted on his dark face, he gave no sign of discomfort. Did he know who she was? Of course he did. He must have known she would be here this morning. That was why he'd smiled so ironically. And she'd given way to a stupid, coy, damned schoolgirl blush—what a complete idiot he must have thought her!

Honor's green eyes turned arctic. Yes, Mr Raven's appearance exactly fitted the mental image she'd had when she'd read that crimson folder. Cold, grim, predatory. Taut as a bowstring, she met the dark gaze again, but this time her face stayed as immobile as a pale mask. What perverse quirk of fate had organised *this* little joke?

There was no kindness in those grimly amused black eyes, no pity at all. The eyes of a man who treated other humans like cattle.

'See what I mean?' Mike mouthed beside her ear. 'He keeps staring at you!'

'Be quiet, Mike' she hissed back.

'Pardon me for living,' he shrugged. She didn't listen to Mark's concluding remarks. Mentally, she was using the kind of words she'd only heard Toby use when he was really upset. If Dominic Raven was going to have anything to do with ComTech, then her life was going to get very difficult. She would never be able to face the man without anger and embarrassment.

'Mr Raven will be making recommendations as he goes along, and we'll try to implement as many of them as we can. Are there any questions at this stage?' Mark asked the assembled company. After a few more seconds' silence, he scooped up his notes. 'Meeting adjourned, then. Thank you all for coming.'

Almost everyone in the room looked slightly stunned as the buzz of conversation rose up. Listening with only half an ear to Mike Wetherall's ironic remarks, Honor rose to her feet. *Damn* it. Why did this have to happen right now?

'What's your hurry?' Mike wanted to know as she scooped up her shoulder-bag and squeezed round the cactus.

'I've got a lot of work to do,' she said briefly.

There was only one exit to the boardroom, and she was determined to be out as soon as possible. To her dismay, though, the press of people leaving forced her to share the doorway momentarily with Ian Thompson, Mark MacDonald, and Dominic Raven.

It was Mark who paused in the atrium outside. 'Honor, hold on a moment. I want you to meet Dominic.' Gritting her teeth, Honor stopped, and met the formidable pair of dark eyes that turned on her. 'Dominic, this is Honor O'Hara, who's now in charge of our sales division,' Mark said, oblivious to any tension in Honor's stance. 'She's been with us for four years, since just after the company began.'

Dominic Raven had the kind of face that under different circumstances would have stopped Honor's heart in its tracks. A ruthlessly male face, the mouth and eyes holding an almost shocking erotic challenge; and yet there was a glitter of humour there, too, which hadn't been evident from across the room.

'Hello, Honor.' His voice was almost exactly as she'd anticipated, deep and virile. Definitely superior, yet not quite mocking enough to be offensive.

'How do you do?' she responded formally to the deep voice. He was holding out his hand, and she couldn't very well ignore it, not with Ian and Mark smiling benignly on. Nervously she gave him her hand, hoping he wouldn't notice how moist her palm was suddenly.

'I've heard excellent things about you,' he said, with the nearest to a smile she'd yet seen on his dark face. But no returning smile came to Honor's lips.

'Really?' she said without warmth. Detestable man!

'Mark speaks very highly of you. You hold a position of considerable trust.'

Her eyes glittered green fire at that. 'Does that arouse your suspicions, Mr Raven?'

It was more of a challenge than a joke, and the deep lines that bracketed his mouth curved still further. 'Should it?' he enquired.

'Hardly. I'm just a very small cog in a big machine. I assure you.'

'You do yourself an injustice,' he said smoothly. 'You handle a great deal of confidential material, Honor.'

'All I see are figures, Mr Raven.'

'But figures are vital, don't you think?' With teasing insolence, his eyes dropped for a moment to study the swell of her breasts against her blouse. Then he smiled directly into her eyes. 'I hope you're going to be able to spare me some time over the next few days, Miss O'Hara. I'm relying on your co-operation.'

'Oh?' It was diffcult to restrain her anger any longer especially as her breasts were now tingling as though his glance had been a wicked male caress across her naked skin. She turned to Mark MacDonald with something like accusation in her green eyes. 'Is my department thought to be compromised, Mark?'

'Of course it isn't,' Mark said a touch impatiently.

'There's no need to be so defensive. But security can always be improved. I've just tried to explain to everyone back there that no one should feel slighted.' His voice became more soothing. 'The whole company policy needs overhauling, Honor. There's no implication that you've failed in any way. Nor you, Mike,' he added to Mike Wetherall, who had been standing silently on the fringe of this conversation.

Honor felt a palpable sense of relief as Dominic Raven turned his attention away from her to be introduced to Mike.

'The whole point,' Mark was going on, 'is to make ComTech more secure. It isn't a witch-hunt. But computing is a highly competitive field, and we need the sort of expert advice Mr Raven can give us ...'

Mark was repeating much of the speech he'd just given in the boardroom, and she and Mike listened in silence. As soon as she could decently do so, Honor excused herself, and left the little group. As she hurried back to her office, she was painfully aware that Dominic Raven's dark eyes were probably following her trim legs.

She was shaking as she slammed her office door behind her, and sank into her chair. God *damn* it! She squeezed her temples hard; they were suddenly aching.

The brief encounter had been distinctly unsettling. Her heart was still pounding as though she'd run a marathon. That hatefully superior, patronising air!

Had he been laughing at her all the while? Challenging her to show any sign of recognition?

The tap at her door heralded Mike Wetherall.

'Well,' he said grimly. 'And what do you make of *that*?'

'It's hardly pleasant.' She drew a breath, intending to tell Mike what had happened between Pru and Mog Lambert, but Mike's anger was spilling over.

'Pleasant? I'll say it's not. Mark might have consulted

with his staff before unleashing all this on us! He's the coldest, most arrogant bastard in town——'

'*Mark?*' Honor blinked.

'Raven,' Mike said. 'He's notorious for thinking himself superior to the whole human race.' He dragged the heavy Yellow Pages across the desk, and flicked through it. 'Ah,' he said, 'I thought so.'

Honor leaned across to study the full-page entry. She recognised the black raven logo from Morgan Lambert's dossier. She gnawed her full lower lip with sharp white teeth as she read the formally laid-out advertisement.

Raven Security handled all aspects of security. Prevention, deterrence, detection, it was all within their scope. They could supply and install their own highly sophisticated equipment for any function from preventing computer fraud to catching burglars.

They could locate missing persons, detect industrial spies, install a closed-circuit TV system, defend your secrets against electonic bugging . . .

Honor shook her head. 'It's quite a list.'

'A very efficient man indeed,' Mike agreed drily. 'If Mr Raven lives up to his advertisement, he must know a great many secrets about a great many people. I wonder whether that's what gives him that superior air?'

'I wonder.' Honor thought again of that strong, ironic mouth, and felt a shudder down her spine. Maybe it wasn't a good idea to tell Mike about Pru just yet, after all. 'That suggestion about a leak—surely it's nonsense?'

'There's a streak of the melodramatic in Mark.' Mike shrugged. 'It's possible, I suppose.'

They discusssed the issue in speculative tones, agreeing in their mutual dislike of the man Mark MacDonald had called in. As they talked, it came to Honor that her overriding physical impression of the man was that he was, quite simply, the most attractive male she'd ever encountered.

'He's certainly impressive,' Mark said grudgingly, as though picking up her thought. 'And not necessarily in a pleasant way.'

'Quite.' Honor glanced at her watch. 'Anyway, I've wasted enough time already, Mike. I've got to get on.'

'Aye aye, boss.' Taking the hint, Mike let himself out, and she got mechanically down to work. She was too upset to concentrate for a few minutes. But her tensions slowly ebbed away, leaving her feeling slightly drained.

Mr Raven's presence here would simply have to be tolerated until he went away. And that was all. Honor O'Hara had deep wells of patience in her character—and that was despite the passionate Celtic nature she'd been born with. Her life had not always been happy, and it had taught her very early to rely completely on herself. She called herself a realist, and indeed, she had a unique capacity of being able to accept what she could not change.

Yet there was always that irrational sense of romance to ruin her best laid plans. Somewhere underneath all the realism lay hope, like a sprouting daffodil under snow, waiting only the faintest encouragement of sun to burst into flower. Even now, despite what Dominic Raven had done to Pru, she still hoped about Mog. Hoped his father would change his mind, hoped that they'd get together some day.

Stupid. There would be no flowers for Pru. Not from Mog—Dominic Raven had seen to that, very effectively.

Despite everything Honor could do, her sister's life seemed to have turned into a desert of loneliness, used tissues, and self-pity.

Painfully, Pru was having to rethink her future. A future that would be without Mog. Everything had once been so simple. After the wedding, a life full of promise and happiness was going to unfold ...

Funny how secure you could feel over a future that was, in reality, so very uncertain.

What did she face now? It didn't do much good to try and convince Pru that she was young, carefree and single again. She was emotionally shattered, and despite the year's salary that Morgan Lambert had given her—guilty generosity?—she was now unemployed. Pru was going to miss Mog acutely, and she was going to miss the secure feeling of having her future all mapped out for her by domestic blessings and exigencies.

Seeing Pru in such a pathetic state made the prospect of future meetings with Dominic Raven all the more bitterly galling.

As it happened, it took a remarkably short time for Dominic Raven's influence to be felt at ComTech.

The first signs were almost ludicrously irritating. Kettles were banned from all offices. 'To stop us steaming other people's letters open,' Mike Wetherall explained with a horrible grin. To her disgust, Honor was forced to give up her beloved Darjeeling tea (one of her few self-indulgences) for the ersatz coffee produced by the newly installed machine in the atrium.

There were other annoyances. Access to all reprographic equipment was now severely restricted. Someone was on duty in the photocopy room all day, and everyone had to sign a register for use of the machines. To Honor, whose confidential secretary Laura needed to copy things several times a day, the restriction was especially tiresome.

Waste-paper bins were also abolished in favour of shredders in several offices. Honor, who handled confidential trading information like profit and loss and cash flow, was one of the first recipients.

'It's starting to feel like a concentration camp in this place,' Laura Skimmington complained bitterly to Honor.

'You should see all the stuff they're bringing into our office this morning. Ultra-violet markers, the lot.'

'I did see some men in overalls carrying equipment through to the typing pool,' Honor nodded.

'That shark pool, more like.' Laura, who had been Honor's own secretary for the past year, pulled a vinegary face, her mauve-rimmed glasses dangling askew on a gold chain. The way Laura's mauve glasses clashed wildly with her dyed red hair had always made Honor somehow very fond of her. 'No one's allowed to just walk into Records any more. You've got to sign a chitty. And look at this.'

She showed Honor a ream of typing paper. Instead of the old-style white Bank stuff, every sheet of the new paper was printed with a complicated, pale green ComTech insignia, almost like a watermark.

'Very smart,' Honor smiled.

'It's supposed to make documents hard to forge and copy.' She tucked her sheaf of green-printed paper under her arm grimly. 'They say he's terrifying.'

'Dominic Raven?'

Laura nodded. 'Why, I don't believe there ever *was* a leak, do you?'

'I'd hate to think there was,' Honor admitted.

'The atmosphere's changing here,' Laura said meaningfully, on her way to the door. 'And not for the better.'

When she next saw Mike, in Joanna Rockley's office, he was elaborating on the same theme.

'It's like working for MI5,' he grumbled, polishing his glasses on his tie. 'Everyone's creeping around shredding their carbon paper. Have you seen the latest menu?'

Honor shook her head.

'This is mine,' Joanna said, passing it to her. 'Yours'll be just the same.'

Honor read it in silence while Joana and Mike watched her glumly over their machine-brewed coffee. It was from

Mark, and it set out a long list of new procedures dealing with access to secure information. More restrictions on everyday life, she thought irritably.

There were three more points overleaf, and she felt her irritation flicker into anger as she read them. Firstly, the telephones of all senior personnel were to be direct-line from now on, bypassing the switchboard. And that was going to mean a lot of wasted time hunting for numbers which she'd always relied on the switchboard to find for her.

Secondly, all desk tops were to be cleared daily from now on, and all offices were to be locked, and the keys given to the porter.

And thirdly, all senior personnel were being asked to complete something called a 'continuous *curriculum vitae*'.

'Personal details,' Joanna interpreted. 'You'll be sent the form any time now, and it's *very* full. They practically want to know what colour knickers you wear on Fridays—and though they're careful to say you don't *have* to fill it in if you don't want to, you can imagine what they'll think if you refuse.'

'But that's outrageous,' Honor said, feeling her skin flush at the memory of that red dossier. Damn Raven! There was something about his style that rasped on your nerves like sharkskin. 'Why should we have to submit to this kind of thing?'

'Why indeed?' Mike said darkly.

'"The essence of commercial security is not hardware, but conditioning the mental processes",' Joanna quoted. 'From the sayings of Dominic Raven, as printed in yesterday's *Financial Times*. He's always in the papers.'

Joanna Rockley, ComTech's liaison officer, worked two offices away from Honor and Mike. At twenty-six, she was very pretty in a blonde, almost teenage way. Mike and Joanna had always been close, flirtatious, even—though she and Honor didn't have much in common. From time to time she'd talked Honor into an occasional visit to the hairdresser or the beauty salon with her, but that was as far as it went. 'He frightens me,' she went on. 'I suppose he'll want to talk to us fairly soon.' She touched each corner of her perfectly made-up mouth with her little finger, an oddly middle-aged gesture, then pulled her jersey taut over pert little breasts. 'Of course, he's rather magnificent in a hateful sort of way.'

'Mark's very easily influenced,' Mike mused over his freshly polished hornrims, 'for all his intelligence . . .'

'*Who's* magnificent?' Honor said snappishly. 'You don't mean Raven?'

'Of course.' Joanna looked surprised at Honor's expression. 'He's a superb figure of a man, you must have noticed. And they say——' She looked as though she'd have said more if Mike hadn't been there. 'He's got that sort of purposeful, intent look, you know . . .'

'The eternal hunter.' Mike supplied drily. 'Roaming the trackless wilderness in search of his quarry while the little woman waits in the cave over the rabbit stew. That sort always seem to get female hormones flowing.

'That's exactly it, yeah,' Joanna nodded eagerly, oblivious to any sarcasm in Mike's tone. 'It's a sort of primitive thing, I suppose.'

Mike bared his teeth at Honor over Joanna's blonde head, and shuffled off to his office. Honour picked up the files she wanted from Joanna, and made her way back to her own room.

Magnificent? The word grated on her, yet she knew it was irrational to be irritated by it. She'd hardly been close enough to Raven to be able to quarrel with the description. She thought again of that entry in the Yellow Pages. *Legal evidence.* Ugh!

Her door was ajar, but that didn't register until she pushed through.

And with a sense of physical shock, found herself staring into the jet-black eyes of the man who'd just been occupying her thoughts. Standing tall and dark against her window, waiting.

The shock made her gasp, and the files slipped through her fingers on to the floor in an untidy heap.

'I was about to give up on you,' he said pleasantly.

She muttered something unintelligible, gulping down her heart. She could feel his eyes on her as she knelt to pick up the files, her heart beating painfully. 'Did I startle you?' he asked innocently.

'Yes,' she replied shortly. Her voice was an unfriendly grunt, partly because of her position at his feet. No doubt he would read all sorts of guilty secrets into her surprise.

'You ought to lock your door when you go out. But I'm sorry if I alarmed you.' He didn't sound sorry in the slightest. 'I've been wanting a word with you for some time, but I haven't had a chance until now.'

'Oh?' she queried coldly, rising to her feet and dumping the files on her desk. Her raven-dark hair had tumbled around her oval face, and she wasn't feeling at her most composed. 'Can I help you in any way?'

'I hope so.' He was even more handsome than she'd remembered. Imperious eyes, passionate mouth, uncompromisingly masculine features, all contributing to a face that was vibrant with life. A supreme male animal with a magnetism that almost overwhelmed you. Joanna had been right, she thought numbly. *Magnificent* described Raven exactly. The kind of man who somehow made you ache just to watch him move. 'Can you spare me a few minutes?' he asked, reclining comfortably into her chair and assessing her with frank interest.

She felt damned awkward standing up in her own office, but since he was occupying the only chair, her only alternative was to perch on the desk. And she was not going to do that.

She picked up her phone, and asked Mike to take any of her calls for the next fifteen minutes, then faced him. 'I'm ready.'

Her challenging manner simply didn't register. His lips parted momentarily to show excellent white teeth. 'By the way, I hope you don't mind my calling you Honor?'

'It's my name,' she said ungraciously.

'It's a very seductive name. Or is that an unpardonably sexist remark?' Sleek muscles shifted under his beautifully cut suit as he rose, fluid as a panther. 'But forgive me. I'm taking your seat.'

Honor moved to his courteous gesture obediently, and sat. For some crazy reaon, though, she felt even less at ease with him standing. He was tall enough to dominate the room, and he filled the air with a kind of dangerous electricity that made her mouth feel dry.

His eyes had moved to the processor on her desk. 'Is that where you do most of your work?'

Honor nodded. The big-format screen was in essence her desk top. He came over to study it, drumming long fingers on the beige plastic cover. 'Just how secure is the system from unauthorised entry?'

'Not very,' Honor shrugged. 'Anyone who's got access to a desk-top terminal can key into the network. But then, it doesn't have to be very secure, does it? No one's interested in ComTech's trading results.'

'That's naïve,' he said coolly.

She sent him an acid-green look from under thick lashes. This man and old Morgan Lambert had the same nasty, suspicious minds. 'Freedom of access to information is what computers are all about, you know.'

'Computers have been the biggest security disaster of this century,' he said with gentle condescension. Why should her stomach quiver just because he smiled into her eyes like that? 'Especially when you consider that most firms are as leaky as sieves anyway.'

'Including this one?' Honor suggested sweetly.

'It could be improved,' he agreed.

'Well, you're doing your best to improve us,' she pointed out with a glint of malice. 'The place is changing so that we hardly know ourselves any more.'

'Perhaps the place, as you call it, needs to be changed.'

'To the extent of making everyone in the firm feel like a potential traitor?' she returned briskly. 'Compiling dossiers on everyone, checking everyone's movements—that's going to do wonders for morale, Mr Raven.'

'The price of freedom is eternal vigilance.' She recognised his expression; the wide-eyed amusement of a big cat playing with a doomed mouse. 'And potential traitors are at least preferable to actual traitors, don't you agree?'

'Ah.' Honor arched a sceptical eyebrow at him, 'You really think someone stole the plans for the LP-550, then?'

'I'm surprised that you don't think so,' he replied calmly.

'What makes you think I don't?'

'The patently disbelieving expression on your velvety mouth,' he said gently. 'But I'm afraid I find it hard to believe in coincidences of that sort, Honor.'

'Perhaps I'm less sophisticated than you are,' she suggested, compressing the velvety mouth in question into an unlovable line.

'Perhaps.' The smoky eyes had dropped to her breasts now. She was dismayed to realise that the near-quarrel with him had hardened her nipples flagrantly against the thin material of her blouse. Hot with embarassment, she folded her arms.

'In any case, I'm beginning to wonder what this all has to do with me.'

'Who knows?' he smiled. 'A beautiful woman can do more to wreck well laid security arrangements than any amount of technology.'

'Are you saying you suspect me?' she snapped incredulously.

'I was merely joking,' he said with amusement. Those dark eyes seemed to touch her all the time, watching her fingers as they moved, savouring the lines of her body under her clothes—or so she couldn't help feeling. 'Don't you like being teased?'

'I don't like people who pry into the lives of others.' she said shortly, the words coming out before she had time to stop them.

'Ah.' Those eyes weren't cold, she realised suddenly. They were warm. Fire, not ice, lay behind them. Was he actually flirting with her? 'Now you confirm my suspicions. You sound like a woman with something to hide.'

'That's the stock response, isn't it?' she shot back. 'A person has to be guilty of something to want to prevent the erosion of what few civil liberties are left these days. If he tries to stop Big Brother from destroying his privacy, he must have something to hide. If he objects to having his phone tapped, or his keyholes spied through, or his family life laid bare for everyone to see, then he must be a subversive, mustn't he?'

'You're very articulate,' Dominic Raven said gently. If anything, his eyes were warmer now, and that infuriated Honor. 'As it happens, I quite agree with you that human rights are steadily being crushed. I see my job as defending those rights, though—not violating them.'

'Oh, please,' she said scornfully. 'At least have the courage of your convictions Mr Raven.'

'You mean, play the devil's part you seem so determined to cast me in?' he enquired, arching one eyebrow. 'I think you've got the wrong end of the stick, Honor. I'm here with the specific brief of defending ComTech's privacy.'

'In between digging up the dirt on private citizens?' she asked ironically, aware that she was growing dangerously close to an outright insult. But he seemed unfazed.

'I'm afraid dirt doesn't interest me,' he said mildly.

'No?' Honor's beautiful mouth expressed some of the acid disbelief she felt inside. 'What's the fashionable line these days? Gathering evidence for divorce cases? Or do you prefer to get your oar in before the wedding even takes place?'

This time she had scored. Hs smile faded slowly as he studied her face with serious eyes. 'What are you talking about?' he asked in a quiet voice.

'You know perfectly well what I'm talking about,' she told him sharply. 'Are you trying to say you don't happen to remember that Prudence O'Hara is my sister?'

'No, I'm not saying that.' There was a stillness about him now, a watchfulness. She was uncomfortably aware of hard, living muscle under his silk suit. He must know how she felt towards him—it was plain sadism to rub it in by prolonging this interview! 'I recognised you the moment I saw you.'

'No doubt. You've had your photographers tailing my family for the past couple of weeks.' Anger made her throw caution to the winds. 'Oh yes, I've seen your report, Mr Raven. It doesn't exactly square with your high-flown ideals, does it?'

A glint of anger was visible for a moment in his eyes. But his voice stayed cool. 'If you mean the report I think you do, then it was a highly confidential document.'

'Oh, don't worry,' she said scathingly, 'there wasn't anything in it I didn't know already, Mr Raven. In fact, Pru and I were both impressed with your thoroughness.'

'You weren't meant to see it. Nor was Prudence. The only person who had a right to see it was the person who commissioned it.'

'You'll be accusing *me* of violating personal privacy next,' she said drily.

'That's exactly what I am doing,' he replied unemotionally. 'How did you come by the report?'

'Your friend Mr Lambert was rather careless with it,' Honor said bitterly.

His eyes clouded slightly. 'That was unfortunate.'

'Yes,' she agreed in the same tone. 'Unfortunate. Like our family circumstances.'

The way his mouth tightened told her he'd recognised her reference. 'You read my letter too, I take it?'

'Oh, yes,' she nodded, 'we were quite shameless. Odd that you should think Prudence *unsuitable* for Mog Lambert, though. She thought *you* were rather nice. But then, she is rather lacking in judgement, isn't she?'

He walked to the window and leaned on the sill, strong, tanned fingers gripping the wood. 'You're an adult woman,' he said quietly. 'You know that even our nearest and dearest would be painfully hurt if they knew everything we said or thought about them. It's even more potentially harmful to take that sort of remark out of context.'

'The *context*,' she retorted, giving the word a bitter slant, 'is my sister's life. As I see it, Mr Raven, Morgan Lambert had some doubts as to whether Pru would make his son a good wife. He asked you to help him make his mind up—and that report you or your minions compiled was enough to make him send Mog off to America by the next flight.' She drew a breath. 'You don't deny that?'

'No,' he said quietly. 'In essence, you're right.'

'Well, Mr Raven, I just wish you could see Prudence right now.' Honor's face was pale and set. 'I wish you'd tell me how to comfort her when she cries herself into exhaustion every night. I wish you'd tell me what to say to her when she feels that her life just isn't worth living any more.'

The silence was tense. When he turned to face her, there

were taut lines around his mouth and eyes, and unless she was very much mistaken, his tanned skin was paler now. 'There isn't anything I can offer,' he said tersely. 'I'm sorry about Prudence. I liked her, too. Shall we stick strictly to business from now on?'

'That suits me fine,' Honor said shortly. She was shaking with angry nerves. At least she'd hit back at him in a tiny way, though it had given her scant satisfaction to do so.

'Good,' he said flatly. 'We'll get back to the internal control system. Can you tell me how it works?'

She tried to keep her voice steady. 'It's like any other business. When a sales order note comes in, we have to verify any credit terms which the rep may have offered. Sometimes they're not acceptable, in which case we either cancel the order, or issue a cash transaction note. Salesmen,' she explained flatly, 'are sometimes a little to keen to make a sale.' With the fluency of someone who understood her job fully, Honor went through the routine, glad to be back on a business footing again. 'The order then gets put on the register. I notify the office down the corridor and the factory stores manager in Kent. Kent prepare the machines for dispatch, usually within twenty-four hours.'

'And then?'

'If the goods are in stock, Kent get back to us to confirm that they're ready for dispatch. We make sure invoices in triplicate get sent to the customer, the stores manager, and the customer file at Finance. The order is dispatched to the retail outlet via the carriers. When that happens, we send the information up to Records, and file the paperwork here.'

He nodded in the direction of the adjoining wall. 'Wetherby does much the same kind of thing?'

'Mike handles mainframe computers. I do all the home computer sales.'

'Is there any reason for that division?'

'It's just the way things turned out,' Honor shrugged. 'We don't build all that many mainframes—just to specific customer orders. Mike knows far more about computer design than I do, so although it's a small field, it needs more applied knowledge.'

'But you're in charge of the division?'

'Yes.'

'I see.' His eyes were thoughtful. 'Is there ever any friction between you?'

'No,' she said shortly. 'Why should there be?'

'He's a few years older than you are, and by your own admission more experienced. Added to which,' he said silkily, 'some men never adjust to working under a woman.'

'Mike seems to have adjusted perfectly well to working under me,' she said coolly. 'And he happens not to be an ambitious person.'

'Whereas you are?' The question was casual. She looked up mutinously, about to deliver some stinging retort, but he didn't let her. 'I'd like to see the very first two weeks' sales figures for the LP-550. Can you print them out?'

Honor nodded, and swung to face her keyboard. Within a few moments, her printer clattered into life, spooling out a large loop of figures. She tore them off for him, and passed them over. He glanced at them, then folded the paper over.

'I won't trespass on your time any longer right now. But I'd like very much to talk to you further about your sister.'

'Haven't we said all there is to say already?' she asked coldly.

'I think not. Will you have lunch with me today?'

Anger ignited in her again. Damn him! Was he really still imagining he could chat her up, after what he'd done? 'Under the circumstances,' she said acidly, 'I hardly think so, Mr Raven.'

'Some other time, then.'

'I think not.'

He moved over to where she sat, and stared down at her intently. 'You're very sure of yourself,' he said softly, in a voice that made her spine tingle. 'Very confident and very hostile. But when you looked into my eyes in that boardroom, I saw something in them which no woman would have allowed to show—if she hadn't meant it.'

She was utterly lost for words. Suddenly, that warm, dominant mouth was frighteningly close. In the panic that he might be about to kiss her, Honor's heart seemed to flip right over inside her chest.

Instead, he reached out to touch her face, smiling into her wide eyes. After her seething anger, the emotional impact of the small gesture hit her like a brick. She simply sat there, her eyelids fluttering closed.

She was overwhelmingly conscious of his power, the touch of his fingers on her cool cheek. For an aching second she submitted to his caress, and then it was over, leaving her as breathless as twenty thousand feet of altitude.

'I wasn't wrong,' he said softly. Unlike her, he was utterly in control. Unlike her, his hands weren't shaking like autumn leaves now. 'I did see it in your eyes. You may think you hate me, Honor. But if you think I intend to give you up without a struggle, you're very much mistaken.'

CHAPTER THREE

'You haven't touched a thing,' Honor chided gently. 'Can I make you something else?'

'It's delicious.' Pru sighed unhappily. 'I just don't feel like eating. I'm sorry, Honor. Maybe it'll keep.'

With a wan smile, Pru got up and lifted her coat off the chair.

'Where are you going, piglet?' Honor asked quietly.

'I promised to see Caroline,' Pru said briefly. Honor knew it was more likely she'd be walking the streets alone, staring at the pavement with unseeing eyes, but she didn't interfere. Let Pru work it out in her own way.

However, she'd wanted her sister's company tonight, for her own selfish reasons; it would have been a relief to get away from confused, dark thoughts of Dominic.

Now, as she cleared the table alone, she was thinking of jet-black eyes, and the shape of a commanding mouth. Dominic's parting words had disturbed her almost more than that threatened kiss. What did he mean by not giving her up without a struggle? Heaven forbid that he'd found her attractive, had set his mind on conquering her! That didn't bear thinking of.

Did she find him attractive? Ugly question. How in God's name could someone you disliked so much affect you so crudely? And *crudely* was the only way to describe it. She felt it every time she thought of him. While her intellect recoiled from Dominic Raven, her body responded with a quivering excitement that was utterly new to her.

It was perverse. No other word for it. To desire

physically what you disliked intellectually was sheer perversity.

It made her feel hot under the collar just to think of Dominic. But she'd felt more alive during that stormy interview than she had done for years.

She roused herself, wondering inconsequentially whether Dominic Raven lived alone. Or with a woman? Probably the latter, given those stunning looks. But if he already had a woman in his life, why had he seemed so intent on Honor O'Hara?

Fighting depression, Honor finished the washing up briskly, and yanked off the pink rubber gloves. She was in her mid-twenties already. Materially, she was comfortable enough. She'd taken out a small mortgage to buy this flat, and it looked lovely, furnished with the antiques that she and Pru had repaired or cleaned up themselves. She didn't need a car, though she enjoyed driving. And there was enough in the bank to be able to indulge herself, in the unlikely event that she ever felt like a self-indulgence of some kind.

But she didn't have much else to show for the past five years out of school; only a family that had stopped being a family years ago—except for Pru. She'd left all her friends—her true friends—back in Ireland, when she was eighteen. And it was too long ago now for her to want to renew any of those old acquaintances. Half of them were married—or unmarried—mothers by now.

Honor didn't usually waste time on self-pity. Tonight she just felt down for some reason. She wandered to the window, and looked down at the peaceful scene outside. The maple trees that overhung the stone wall of the garden beyond gave it a secluded, almost countrified air. She wondered absently where Pru was, how she was feeling now . . .

The intrusion of a gleaming black Porsche was

unexpected. It rumbled into the mews, its headlights scything across the stone wall like searchlights, and turned by the iron railings. The engine continued to murmur under her window for a moment, and then cut out.

She knew immediately who it was as he got out, the heavy sheepskin jacket adding bulk to his height. Her heart was pounding unpleasantly as she drew back from the window in haste.

Dominic Raven. Thank God Pru wasn't here! It occurred to her to simply not answer the doorbell, but she knew that was childish. Instead, she turned to the mirror, and tried to compose herself. She pulled the glossy swathe of her black hair into some semblance of elegance. There was nothing she could do about the blue jeans and soft burgundy sweater she'd put on after getting back from work.

The bell ding-donged insistently. Feeling horribly unprepared to face him, she pulled her sweater straight, and opened the door, her mouth dry.

'Good evening.' The sheepskin jacket was hand-made, and beautifully cut, and the upturned collar framed his face in a way that made her heart skip a beat. Black eyes glittered their dangerous challenge. 'May I come in?'

'You can't stay long,' she said curtly. 'Pru will be back soon, and I don't want her to see you.'

The glint in his expression showed how unaccustomed Dominic Raven was to being treated so cavalierly. 'I'll be brief,' he said silkily.

Honor let him in grudgingly, and closed the door behind him. He was so big that he made her flat look cramped, bringing in an eddy of cold, fresh air.

'Very nice.' He was surveying the room with calm thoroughness. 'That painting's a Kostler, isn't it?'

'Yes,' she gritted.

'And that one's a French. A very good French.' Dark

eyes glanced at her casually. 'Your salary must be better than I realised.'

'I'm not financing my art collection by selling secrets, don't worry,' she said acidly. 'As it happens, I bought most of those pictures several years ago, before the artists got famous. I couldn't afford them now.'

'You have excellent taste. But that's what I expected.'

'Did you now?' She was standing with feet together and arms folded, a pose that was hardly welcoming. 'But then you know so much about us. Have you come to do some more research?'

'Not exactly.' She found herself staring up nervously into his tanned face from inches away. He smelled of leather and expensive aftershave. 'You sounded very Irish there. Do you always sound Irish when you're nervous?' He leaned down and kissed her before she could flinch away. For a moment her soft curves were enclosed in his arms, and then she was pushing away furiously, her cheeks flaming.

'You take a lot of things for granted,' she gasped, eyes blazing like angry emeralds. 'Keep your distance, Mr Raven. And the sooner you stop patronising me about my taste, or my efficiency, or my competence, the better!'

'Please,' he reproved gently. 'Dominic.' He pulled off his jacket and dropped it casually on to a chair. He was wearing black underneath it, to match the Porsche. And his eyes. A black jersey that hugged the hard, fit lines of his arms and shoulders; black slacks which emphasised slim hips and long, muscular legs; and soft black leather boots which had probably cost as much as she earned in a month. The only jewellery he wore was a gold Rolex. Security, she reflected drily, must pay very well indeed.

'What can I do for you?' she asked, making it sound as cold as she possibly could.

'You can listen,' he replied, one fist on his hip. 'Are you prepared to?'

'Five minutes,' she clipped out. 'If Pru sees you here, she'll be badly upset.'

'Five minutes, then.' The deeply chiselled line of his mouth curved into a smile. 'But you don't listen with folded arms and clenched teeth, Honor. That indicates prejudice.' He took her arm, and led her to the sofa, his strength too massive and assured to argue with. He sat her down far too close to him for comfort, so close that she could feel the warmth of his body radiating out to her. It made her head swim to look into his eyes, so she looked at his hands instead. Strong, elegant hands, the tanned skin etched with black hair.

'The first point I want to clear up may seem a very minor one to you, but it isn't to me: my firm didn't compile that dossier for Morgan Lambert.'

'Really?' Honor asked with insulting incredulity.

He smiled briefly. 'Really. I expect your sister's told you that I'm not only security consultant to Lambert Exports, but that the family are friends of mine—which is why Morgan Lambert asked me to commission that investigation. I sub-contracted it out to a firm who specialise in that sort of work. I don't investigate private citizens, and I *never* deal with domestic problems.'

'Oh, I'm sure you employed some tame weasel to do the dirty work,' she nodded, her curving mouth expressing some of the weary disbelief she felt inside. 'You just put your name on the notepaper and collect the fee. What difference does it make?'

'I said you'd think it a minor point,' he reminded her gently. 'But it might make a difference to the way you see my firm.'

'And consequently,' she interpreted, 'to the way I see *you*?'

'Sharp, Miss O'Hara,' he said ruefully. 'Yes, that, too.'

'And why should my feelings towards you have the slightest bearing on anything?' she challenged.

The barb bounced off his hide. 'Raven Security is a very

big, very successful firm, Honor. I supply expertise and equipment to some of the most famous companies in Britain. Household names.' He said it without vanity, but without modesty, either. 'I deal with businesses, Honor. Not individuals. Industrial counter-espionage, security systems for premises and communication networks, managing and controlling defence grids—that's my field. I just want you to understand that.'

'You said that was your first point. What's your second?' she enquired coldly. She wasn't in the slightest bit mollified by his disclaimer, and her expression said as much.

'I saw your sister walking down the lane a few minutes ago. Is she still very upset?'

'Considering that you spent some time assessing her character while masquerading as a friend,' Honor said relentlessly, 'you ought to know.'

For a moment his eyes glinted, and then the old, smooth smile touched the corners of his mouth. Absently, she wondered just what it would take to unruffle that massive calm.

'My second point,' he said gently, 'might seem even less pertinent to you.'

'Go ahead.'

'There was nothing in that report except the literal truth.' He noted the way her brows curved angrily down, and held up his hand. 'The facts, Honor, coupled with a few very logical deductions. Prudence wasn't slandered in any way.'

'Now who's being naïve?' Honor retorted. 'The facts aren't always the truth. All that report said about my father was that he was an alcoholic. It didn't mention that he was a gentle, loving man who never in his life did a soul any harm.' She glared at him with bright green eyes, her high cheekbones flushed. 'All you could find to say about my brother was that he was unemployed and had a criminal record. What about the *facts* that he's a brilliant wood-worker, a sensitive, artistic person, and a boy who's had a tragic life?'

'I didn't make that report, Honor,' he reminded her quietly. 'But to answer your question, the facts in the report were the ones Morgan Lambert wanted to get hold of. And before you go on, you might reflect that Morgan Lambert may have had some right to know a little about his future daughter-in-law's family. Just how and when were she and Mog expecting the old man to find out?'

Honor looked uncomfortable. 'Mog was going to let him find out some time after the wedding.'

'And Prudence thought that was reasonable idea?'

'Mog said that once his father got to know Pru . . .'

Dominic arched one dark eyebrow as she tailed off. 'Morgan Lambert is a friend, but he's also the biggest snob in London. From the moment his son announced his engagement to your sister, the whole thing was on a sticky wicket. It was only a matter of time before he made enquiries about her background.' He moved towards her, making her uncomfortably aware of the hard muscles beneath his expensive clothes. 'It didn't occur to you that Mog and Prudence ought to have anticipated any of this?'

Honor twisted away from the truth of that comment. 'You told Morgan Lambert that Mog's marrying my sister would be very unwise,' she accused. 'To me it's inconceivable that anyone could stop a marriage just because one of the parties has "unfortunate family connections"!'

'Prudence's family connections were *not* the reasons I thought the wedding would be unwise,' Dominic said sharply.

Honor stopped short. 'What possible reasons could you have, then?'

'I felt that Prudence was far too young, for one thing. For another, she struck me as very frivolous and self-indulgent, and lacking any real understanding of the seriousness of marriage.' His eyes held hers inexorably. 'And for a third, I believe that her feelings towards Mog Lambert are not as deep as his for her.'

Honor's cheeks had paled. 'How dare you?' she said tensely. 'Prudence has been through hell these past weeks! *You* think *she's* lacking in feeling? What the hell would you know about it, Mr Raven? I doubt whether you've had a real feeling in your life!'

'I may have been wrong in some respects,' he said, a dangerous light in his eyes now. 'But if we come to that, Mog Lambert's feelings can't have been overwhelmingly profound either—or he wouldn't have allowed himself to be packed off without a murmur of protest.'

'You've had your five minutes,' she decided, too angry to trust herself to sit next to him for much longer without wanting to scratch that devastating face.

'Hold on.' He pulled her back down again effortlessly. 'I make it only three.'

'I'm not going to sit here and listen to your spurious self-justifications,' she warned him. 'Mog had no choice. His father threatened to disinherit him!'

'He didn't need his father's money. No man does.'

'You'd have chucked up five million pounds?' she sneered.

'For a pair of green eyes,' he smiled. 'Maybe. I don't even know how much I'm worth, Honor. But I could walk away from the whole thing tomorrow, and know that in three years' time I'd have made back every penny.'

'Oh, bully for you!' she snapped. 'Mog's not like that.'

'So it seems.' With a wicked glint, Dominic tapped her knee. 'I'll tell you something interesting. Mog's father has had himself proposed for a knighthood.'

'Mr Lambert?'

'Sir Morgan Lambert. That has a ring to it, I'd say. It

means being able to climb out of the merely rich bracket, and into the Top People's bracket. And perhaps that may explain why he's so concerned about his son's connection, don't you think? And maybe that's why Prudence's dear Mog was so willing to let himself be shipped off to New York, eh?'

Honor sat in silence, her hands tightly clasped in her lap. If it were true about the knighthood, then Mog would have had all the more reason to want to obey his father's wishes. Yet . . .

'I'd rather not talk about it any more,' she said tiredly.

'We'll talk about something else, then.' He reached out to brush away a strand of her dark hair, an oddly intimate gesture. 'Tell me about your father's drinking, instead.'

'Look it up in the dossier!'

'Paddy always had a weakness for whiskey, did he?' He tilted her mutinous chin up so he could look into her eyes. 'The old Irish failing?'

'If you must know,' she defended her father, 'he never got over my mother's death.' Her voice was uneven, and she cursed the wetness that was making her eyes dim. She didn't want him to know how close to tears she was. 'He drank because he was lonely and grieving, that's all.'

Dominic's touch became gentle. 'Is that when he started drinking?' he asked quietly. 'When your mother died?'

'I don't want to talk about it.'

'I think you should,' he said gently.

'It's none of your business!'

'Whose business is it, then? Tell me about it. Please.'

'Oh, damn!' she said explosively. 'Yes, it was when my mother died.'

'Was it out of control right from the start?'

'No.' She shook her head tiredly. 'That happened when we moved from Dublin to London, four years later. He couldn't hold down a job for more than a few months at a time, and then he just couldn't hold down a job at all.' She gave him an oblique look. 'Are you satisfied now?'

'What made him take all of you away from Ireland?'

'I think he just wanted to get away . . .' She knew now that she wanted to talk about it all to someone, even to Dominic. Her anger against him seemed to have died away. Now he was just someone big and strong, who gave the impression, no matter how delusive, that he cared.

Those early years in London had been hateful. She had still been missing her mother dreadfully, and the strange, rainy city, vaster in a way that Dublin never was, had seemed like a huge prison to the eighteen-year-old girl.

On top of everything, Toby had first started going wrong then. At nineteen, he'd been impossible, quarrelling with her father night and day. He'd fallen in with a wild set of kids, and had been arrested for drugs. The family had simply fallen apart, and she'd felt that her world was coming to an end.

Dominic listened in silence as she tried to tell him what it had been like, black eyes holding hers as though living through every word she was saying.

'What happened in the end?' he asked quietly.

'Toby left home,' she told him. 'He lives in Earl's Court now. I went to boarding school with Pru for my A-levels. And then Daddy died suddenly, two years go. His heart hadn't ever been strong, and with the drink . . .' She tailed off, letting him guess the rest. 'So the house had to be sold, and I moved here with Pru.'

'Boarding school?' he queried. 'That has a depressing ring about it.'

'It was fairly horrible,' she shrugged painfully. 'But much worse for Prudence. She was always very vulnerable.'

'And that's where you started taking care of her,' Dominic guessed.

'I've got an abiding memory of Pru at that school. A little pale-faced girl with sad eyes, in a gloomy black uniform.' Honor glanced up at Dominic. 'She looked like a small, frightened animal. I was all she had in those days.'

'Well, she's blossomed into a beauty now,' Dominic smiled.

Mentioning Pru had brought her out of the past again, into the hostilities of the present. It had hurt to tell him so much about herself, and she ached inside. Yet it had also been a deep relief to say things which she'd never said to a living soul before.

'Wasn't there anything that might have helped your father?' he asked, brooding over what she'd told him.

'Maybe if he'd married again——' She made a futile little gesture. 'Pru and I often thought it would have stopped his drinking. And there were plenty of women who wanted to marry him in Dublin.' She gave Dominic a bittersweet smile. 'He was once a fine-looking man. He just wasn't interested. He didn't want any other woman after Mum.'

Dominic grunted, and fell silent. Against her prejudices, she felt that this big, hard man had been genuinely moved by what she'd told him. Something had imperceptibly softened the harsh lines of his face, and the expression in those dark eyes was no longer glittering and hard, but somehow cloudy.

But he hadn't either paid her the dubious compliment of compassion, or the outright insult of pity—and for that she was grateful.

His eyes lifted to hers, catching her gaze on his face, and he smiled.

'What on earth made you choose computers as a living, Honor?'

Instant bristles replaced her momentary softening towards him. 'You've got a talent for patronising people, haven't you?' she said shortly. 'I went into computers because they happened to interest me rather more than dolls and prams and recipes for strawberry shortcake!'

'I didn't mean to impugn your intelligence,' he said, looking more amused than rebuked. 'You just strike me as a very human, artistic person—and computing is a very clinical, scientific world.'

'That shows you don't know much about computers,' she retorted. 'Computing can be just as exciting as any other line of work, and a darn sight more interesting than most. Anyway,' she shrugged, 'my job is administrative. I don't do much programming.'

'Presumably you studied computers at college?'

'For three years,' she nodded, her expression still unforgiving.

'Let me guess,' Dominic invited. 'You were—and remain—highly motivated, partly because of your background. You worked damned hard at college, had hardly any fun at all, and got top-grade results. With those, you walked straight into a good job with ComTech, despite your youth and relative inexperience. That same capacity for dedicated hard work has made you a sales manager by twenty-five. Am I right?'

'You'd only have needed to ask Mark to find all that out,' she sniffed.

'I haven't asked Mark anything about you.'

'Ah. The poking and prying has yet to begin, then.'

'Now you're being offensive,' he said gently.

'Am I?' she challenged. 'What about this so-called "continuous *curriculum vitae*" of yours? Isn't that going a bit far, even for you?'

'At the risk of boring you with repetition,' he said coolly, 'that is standard practice in many big companies.'

'It's unwarranted prying into people's private lives,' Honor snorted. 'Why on earth should we submit to it?'

'If you don't want to fill the forms in,' he pointed out, 'then you don't have to. No one's forcing you.'

'Except that anyone who doesn't fill in the forms attracts instant suspicion!'

'Your innocence is rather refreshing,' he said with infuriating condescension. 'Look, Honor, a big company is like an extended family. The primary requirement is for absolute honesty between everyone concerned. It can't be an infringement of anyone's liberty merely to ask them to be honest.'

'We've had this argument before,' Honor said warily, beginning to regret having bared her heart to him just now. She had acquired far too much respect for Dominic Raven's formidable brain to get involved in another abstruse discussion with him. She had a feeling that it would take him less than five minutes to convince her that black was white, and up was down. 'My point is that your style is abrasive, Mr Raven. Your approach may be thoroughly up-to-date, and you can probably make a very convincing argument for all the changes you're implementing. But they grate on the nerves. And in a closely knit firm like ComTech, the sort of things you are doing serve only to sow resentment and suspicion. They aren't necessary——'

'If they weren't necessary, then I wouldn't be wasting my time implementing them,' he cut in with the first hint of real anger she'd seen from him. And before she could counter-thrust, he raised a warning hand. 'Let's not argue about it now, Honor. That isn't what I came for.'

'No,' she agreed heavily. 'You came to justify yourself about what you did to Pru.' She met his eyes briefly. 'Justifying yourself about what you're doing to ComTech can come later, can't it?'

A hint of weariness touched his deeply carved mouth. 'Why do we always end up on opposite sides of the fence?'

'Maybe because we start on opposite sides to begin with.'

'Maybe.' He touched her cheek unexpectedly. 'Honor, I know you think you hate me. But will you promise me something? If you ever need any help—with your family, or anything else—will you get in touch with me, first?'

'What makes you so concerned about me?' she asked with a disillusioned smile. 'Does it salve your conscience?'

'I'm interested,' he smiled. 'And I happen to know my way around the law by now. But I don't have a conscience. Least of all about you.'

'That must be a convenient deficiency in your line of business,' she suggested.

'Oh, come on.' His deep voice was like a velvety caress. 'Don't you think you're over-reacting slightly?'

'Over-reacting?'

He took her shoulders in strong hands, thumbs rubbing soothingly across her tensed muscles. She knew she should pull away, but somehow he'd disarmed her. 'You look tired and sad, green eyes. Are you worried about your sister?'

'Yes,' she said. 'You're very wrong, though you think yourself so clever. She loves him, you know.' His fingers tightened momentarily, their strength like steel, and then he laughed huskily.

'Love.' Taking advantage of the way her anger had been defused, he drew her against him, arms encircling her in a warm, powerful band. She could feel the hard strength of his body, and her head sank weakly against his shoulder, his sheer male presence overwhelming her for a moment. 'Tell me,' he commanded, his lips so close to her cheek that she felt the hot touch of his breath, 'have you ever been in love?'

'No.' Her voice was husky, her heart starting to pound against her chest.

'No?' He kissed the satiny skin of her neck, beneath her ear, an almost unbearably erotic caress. 'Then how would you recognise it in someone else?'

'I know how Pru feels!'

'But feelings are treacherous. Would you settle for plain desire?'

She was trembling as she looked up at him. His eyes were hooded, smoky with what he was feeling for her. She didn't need to be told what it was; in that moment she knew she'd never been so completely desired by any man in her life before. Dominic's passions ran deep, wide and strong; to be caught up in that river would be overwhelming, unforgettable.

'I don't understand what you're saying,' she whispered unevenly, the alarm bells of danger ringing wildly in her head.

'Of course you do.' He brushed her temples with his lips, touching her eyelids, her cheeks, the corners of her mouth with insistent tenderness. 'If you understand Prudence, you must understand me. You must have known how I felt about you, from the first time we set eyes on each other.'

'You're mistaken!' She looked up at his mouth, feeling utterly helpless. A carved, beautifully male mouth, strong and passionate and sexy. 'As a matter of fact——'

'Hush!' Her mouth yielded to his like a flower as he pulled her close to him.

His body was alive with muscle, lean and taut with mature strength, and its contact was devastating against her slim curves. Dominic's kiss was dizzying, a pagan assault on her senses which urged her to surrender, here and now. She struggled for freedom like a drowning woman, but he was far too strong, too determined. As his hands caressed the hot skin of her flanks under her sweater, she whispered his name, for the first time.

'Dominic ...' It tasted sweet on her tongue, like a forbidden wine. She clung to him as he unfastened her bra, his palms sliding across her ribs to cup the aching swell of her breasts, his fingers appraising the rigid peaks of her nipples. She whimpered at the electric jolt of pleasure his touch gave her, her mouth seeking his with a flaring hunger of her own now.

His hands were wickedly expert, their strength becoming achingly gentle as he smoothed the full curves of her breasts.

'You're beautiful,' he said softly, eyes black as night on her. 'And you smell so sweet, the way a woman should . . .'

Her legs were weak, her mind spinning. What was she doing? God help her!

And yet as he kissed her again, crushing her hungrily in his arms, she knew that deep inside she'd wanted him from the moment their eyes had met, exactly as he'd guessed.

She needed him with a desperate concentration, her fingers sliding underneath his silk shirt with shameless urgency. His skin was smooth as velvet, but hot to the touch, and his body had the hard strength that only long hours of exercise could bring. Honor arched to him like a bow in a hunter's fingers, her palms tracing the muscles of his back in passionate caresses.

'*Honor!*'

Pru's voice, frightened and breathless, cut into the swirling of her emotions like a knife.

'Pru?' Honor sat up, her hair tumbled across her flushed cheeks like a raven's wing, to see Prudence standing in the doorway, her face pale with shock. Her brown eyes glanced in horror from Honor's face to Dominic's, and then she turned with a choked sob, and ran from the room.

Honor turned on Dominic with tearful eyes, sanity returning through her whirling emotions. 'Damn you! Are you satisfied now?'

'Hardly,' he said with silky sarcasm.

'You should never have come here,' she accused shakily. 'I wish you would just leave me and my family alone!'

'I rather forgot myself,' he said with a dry smile. 'It wasn't difficult.'

'What am I going to say to Prudence?' Honor anguished, trying to restore order to her clothes.

'I don't think you'll have to do much explaining to her,' Dominic observed calmly. His expression was unreadable as he watched her get up shakily from the couch. She pushed her hair back, her mouth dry with the passion she'd just experienced. Pru had been wandering the empty streets alone—while here at the flat she'd been sensually wallowing in the arms of the man who'd wrecked her sister's happiness.

'You're the most destructive man I've ever met,' she said in a low voice. 'Can't you do anything except hurt people?'

'It seems not.' An expression of irony had settled over his dark features. He rose to pull on his jacket, and Honor waited for him to leave, every fibre tensed. Nothing quite as awful as this had ever happened to her. Her veins were still throbbing with Dominic's lovemaking, the melting wetness in her loins telling her how much she'd wanted him. How on earth was she ever going to explain this to Pru? 'I'm going to see my sister,' she said breathlessly, and ran out of the room, leaving him to find his own way out.

Pru was lying on her bed, crying into the pillow. Biting her lip hard, Honor sat down beside her, and stroked the chestnut swathe of her sister's hair.

'H-has he gone?' Pru asked without looking round.

'He's going,' Honor nodded. 'Pru, I'm sorry about that——'

'What was he *doing* here? I hate him!'

Honor tried to soothe her. 'Forget him. Forget he ever came here.'

'How can I forget? He was making love to you!' Pru stared up at her for a moment, pretty face marked with tears, then rolled to face the wall. 'How could you let him kiss you?' she accused, her voice muffled by the pillows. 'After what he did to me?'

Honor looked up to see Dominic standing silently in the doorway. His jacket was slung over his shoulder, watchful eyes intent on her. He looked tall, proud, all gentleness gone from him now. She met his gaze with an expression of contempt, then bent over Pru again, laying her cheek on her sister's shoulder. 'Don't cry,' she murmured softly. 'It doesn't matter.' Let Dominic Raven see the results of his handiwork, the helpless tears of the woman whose feelings he had deemed shallow and unworthy!

When she next looked up, the doorway was empty. The angry growl of the black Porsche rose up from the street outside. She heard him turn the car in the lane, the engine rumbling out of earshot and into the night.

'I don't *understand*,' Pru whimpered. 'What was he doing here? He's dangerous, Honor! He'll hurt you!'

'I know that now,' Honor said tightly. 'He came here to try and explain about that file, Pru. I didn't want to let him in, but I thought I ought to hear what he had to say. Then——' For once in her life, Honor's fluid articulateness wasn't up to an explanation. 'I—I don't quite know what happened then . . .'

'Explain about the file?' Pru rolled on to her back, and looked up at Honor with reddened eyes. 'What did he say?'

'That he didn't compile the report.'

'Course he did! He's a spy, Honor. A smooth, smiling spy!'

'Be that as it may,' Honor said gently, 'he said that some other company made the report, and I think I believe him. He also said that Morgan Lambert's being recommended for a knighthood, and that was why he'd been prompted to investigate your background. Snobbery.'

Pru absorbed that in silence. Her tear-reddened eyes were on Honor's face, and Honor had a sudden feeling that some intimacy between them had been destroyed tonight. With a flicker of fury against Dominic, she wondered when that wary, hurt look would ever fade from her sister's eyes.

'Don't look at me like that,' she said gently. 'It won't happen again, Pru. It was a horrible mistake.'

'How do you know him, anyway?'

'Well . . .' Honor rubbed her cheeks wearily, her mind still branded with red-hot images of Dominic. The excitement she'd felt was curdling into a dull ache in her stomach, and the depression that had threatened earlier this evening was gathering blackly around her. 'Mark's asked him to tighten up security at ComTech. That's how I met him.'

'Oh no,' Pru said dismally.

'It isn't that bad,' Honor tried to smile.

'It's terrible,' Pru sat up urgently. 'You must have nothing to do with him, Honor. Don't let him near you, or he'll destroy you!'

'That's a little melodramatic,' Honor smiled gently, stroking Pru's hair. 'But I'll do my best to keep out of his way. Believe me, I want to see him as little as you do.'

'Then why were you kissing him?'

'He's a very forceful man,' she said dully. 'He—he wants me. God knows why, but he does.'

'He's got some deep, horrible reason, you can be sure of that,' Pru said fiercely. 'Do you care for him?'

'No, not in that sense . . .'

'You *do* care for him,' Pru accused. 'I can see it in your eyes!'

'You're worn out,' Honor soothed.

'If you take up with Dominic Raven,' Pru threatened, 'I'll never forgive you, Honor.'

'It's time you went to bed. Now stop worrying about things that will never happen.' Gently, Honor ushered Pru towards her bedroom. 'Because they never will.'

* * *

Later, lying in the darkness of her bedrooom, Honor tried to relax. What a bloody awful night! It had taken ages to pacify Pru. She felt as though her emotions had been deliberately bruised. She should never had even let Dominic into the flat . . .

She tried to think through what had happened in the past few hours, but it was so confused.

Dominic's passion for her had been almost frightening. And she had no idea how deep it went, whether it stopped at the level of pure sex, or whether he had some darker or deeper motive . . .

What in God's name made him want her? She didn't have enough to attract a man like Dominic, a man who could have any woman he chose, and who had probably already had dozens. He was too much for her.

Nothing and no one would ever control him. And part of his attraction for her—because he *did* attract her, and it would be blind to deny it—was his protectiveness.

She'd known other men, but none like Dominic. He was rough enough and tough enough to make her safe in any situation, and that drew her in some primaevally feminine way. Raven Security, indeed!

I could walk away from the whole thing tomorrow, and know that in three years' time I'd have made back every penny.

That was no idle boast, she knew instinctively. He could do it any time he wanted to.

Sexually, too, he was very different from any other man she'd met. She'd know that from the moment their eyes had met across the boardroom. A dominant male, as ruthlessly virile as a stud stallion, the kind of man most women only dreamed about. Was that what she wanted? A possibly searing encounter with a magnificent lover, who might very well abandon her once she'd been conquered, and leave her aching for him for the rest of her days?

And she had so many reasons to hate him. Not just for

what he'd done to Pru and Mog. Not just because they disagreed on almost everything. Not even just because what he represented was antipathetic to her nature. But because of a fundamental opposition of personalities. Honor was a deeply feminine woman, she knew that, recognised her own woman's nature. And Dominic was utterly male.

And despite what the sentimental magazines said, there was a gulf between those two states that was almost too wide to be bridged.

Except in bed. She curled on her side, feeling the need for him still alive in her veins, like some dangerous drug that had been flooded into her system. Physically, her need for him was free of any doubts. She ached for him, arms and breasts and womb, ached for him to fill her . . .

She didn't want to think about it any longer. There were no conclusions to come to, no easy answers. She just wanted to sleep now.

But sleep was a long time in coming. And the dreams it brought, when it did come, were of a nature as to make insomnia preferable.

CHAPTER FOUR

HONOR's thoughts were clearer when she awoke the next morning. As she opened her eyes, a phrase was running through her dreams. *Just as well . . .*

She clambered out of the pitch-pine four-poster Toby had made her as a birthday present last year, and opened her lacy bedroom curtains, letting in the dawning of a bright spring day. The sky was an almost impossibly clear eggshell blue, with not a cloud in sight. With luck, it would be warm today.

She showered, still trying to resolve the riddles she'd set herself last night. *Why* in heaven's name had she let Dominic go so far with her? It was difficult, soaping her neat breasts and flat stomach, not to remember the way his lovemaking had devastated her last night. Just touching the places he'd touched last night had set them throbbing again.

He wouldn't be in the same vulnerable state this morning, she thought wrily. His man's body was hard, like his man's character. It didn't take impressions. Why was she so soft? she cursed . . .

She peeped in at Pru. She was still sleeping soundly, but her face was stained with tears, like a child's, and the tangled state of her bedclothes testified to nightmares and insomnia.

Damn!

Poor little kid. Honor decided not to wake her for breakfast, but let her sleep on while she let herself out of the flat, and made her way to work.

She bumped into Margaret Lindsay, the cleaning contractor's supervisor, in the corridor outside the lift in the

Cromwell Centre. She was wearing a large green badge marked VISITOR. Honor inspected it with a frown.

'What does that mean? You're from outer space?'

'New regulations,' Mrs Lindsay smiled. 'Everyone has to wear them from now on.'

'This place really *is* becoming a prison,' Honor commented sourly.

'I wouldn't say that.' Margaret Lindsay tucked her ample bosom behind her clipboard. 'ID badges are in force with a lot of our clients these days. Don't forget, the staff has tripled here since I first started coming. You have to be able to tell the strangers from the employees,' she nodded judiciously. 'Computers are a vulnerable industry. I mean, someone might steal the secret formula, or something.'

Honor sighed a reluctant agreement. Dominic's influence was pervading the whole building, like a kind of invisible fog. 'I hear Mr MacDonald's got Raven Security sorting you all out?' Mrs Lindsay said chirpily. '*Such* a good company. And what a gentleman Mr Raven is! His people did the security for our premises after the burglary. Marvellous job. Alarms on the windows and the doors, pressure-pads under the carpets—it's so safe not even a mouse could get in now. But I don't have to bother about it at all. They've fixed it so I just switch it on as I go out, and bingo!'

'Bingo,' Honor agreed wrily. 'He's a very efficient gentleman. See you, Mrs Lindsay.'

Her own ID card was among the mail on her desk. A thin plastic square, complete with a photograph of herself. The note from Mark that came with it requested her to wear it at all times inside the building.

She was pinning the badge glumly to her lapel when the phone on her desk rang. Since the direct line had been installed she'd been getting all the calls the switchboard would have fielded before, and it was adding to her workload.

'Honor O'Hara.'

'How is your sister this morning?'

Honor recognised the deep, rich voice at once. 'Rather drawn,' she said with no trace of warmth in her reply. 'She spent a bad night.'

'I'm sorry to hear that, Honor. Will she be all right?'

Unmollified by this show of compassion, Honor told him shortly, 'She'll live.'

'I'm also sorry that she saw what she did,' Dominic said calmly. 'It must have been something of a surprise for her.'

'"Shock" would be a better word, I think.' At least, she was thinking, you've got some idea what you've done to her now. 'Prudence is at a rather sensitive stage of her life just now. And she tends to associate you with what happened to her.'

'A pity,' he said easily, dismissing the topic with no audible emotion.

'You should never have come round,' she accused, feeling that something a lot more sincere in the way of an apology was required. 'It was callous and thoughtless.'

He ignored the hint. 'And you? Did you sleep well?'

'Very well, thank you,' she said shortly. 'As it happens, I was just thinking of you, Mr Raven.'

'Indeed?' he purred.

'Yes. I was just pinning my nice, shiny new ID badge on to my lapel.'

Her vinegary tone brought a huskily intimate laugh drifting into her ear. 'Ah! In which case, your thoughts won't have been of a very favourable kind?'

'Not exactly,' she admitted drily.

'Not favourable enough to come out with me tonight?' Taken aback at his effrontery after what had happened last night, Honor was momentarily lost for a reply. He cut through the silence smoothly. 'Given that you're interested in modern art, I thought you might like to go to the new Panovka exhibition. It opens tonight at the Cloth Market.

I'm one of the sponsors, so I have a couple of complimentary tickets. Will you come with me?'

Honor tapped her pencil nervously on her desk. 'I'm afraid I can't go anywhere with you tonight, Mr Raven——'

'I realise it's unforgivably short notice,' he interrupted her gently. 'But it would mean a lot to me to think I could make up, in some way, for last night. And it won't take up a great deal of your time. A couple of hours, no more. Cocktails and snacks—and I could introduce you to the great man himself, if you liked . . .'

His voice tailed off invitingly, and Honor bit her lip in frustration. Getting involved any further with Dominic was going to make for a very complicated relationship with Pru. But the thought of seeing him had started the blood racing along her veins—and quite apart from that, she really did want to go to the new Ivan Panovka exhibition; and it wasn't all that often that she was invited out anywhere these days . . .

'Of course,' Dominic put in conversationally. 'Panovka is one of the few truly great modern painters. Would you call him a genius?'

'I suppose I would,' she ventured. 'He's certainly a marvellous draughtsman . . .'

'I agree. This new exhibition is quite a radical departure for him, I believe. It's as rare opportunity to see a major painter changing direction.'

'It *would* be fascinating,' she heard herself saying reluctantly.

'Good,' he said, as though her ungracious tone had been the warmest acceptance. 'Shall I pick you up at seven sharp?'

'Not at the flat.' She was already regretting her moment of weakness, but it was too late now. 'I'll wait for you at the bottom of the lane.'

'I'll wait for *you*,' he said softly. 'I can't wait to see you again, green eyes.'

The tone of his voice had raised the golden down on Honor's forearms into goose-flesh. She had a sudden vision of that warm, intoxicating mouth.

'If you're planning to repeat last night's performance,' she warned him, 'you can forget the whole thing!' She'd meant to sound sharp, but it had come out shrill. Self-consciously, she lowered her voice. 'Paintings, yes. Seduction, no.'

'You make me sound like some kind of Don Juan,' he said with velvety laughter in his voice. 'But I'll try and keep my primitive instincts in check. Art for art's sake. I promise.

The fact that the Cloth Market was one of London's most prestigious galleries hadn't stopped it from almost going bankrupt in recent years. The intervention of a consortium of top business people had saved it—and, by the way Dominic was being treated tonight, she thought wrily, his contribution must have been one of the biggest.

Housed in a beautiful eighteenth-century building that had once been the centre of the silk trade in London, the ornate rococo plasterwork and chequerboard marble floors formed an elegant backdrop for the obviously well heeled party tonight. Devoid of a fur or diamonds, Honor felt quite under-dressed.

But the whole scene made an odd contrast with the clean, hard modernity of Ivan Panovka's latest work.

'When you said he'd changed direction,' she murmured in some amusement to Dominic, 'I didn't think it would be as completely as *this*. As I remember, his last exhibition was all religious works.'

'I think his life must have taken a somewhat different turning since then,' Dominic agreed. His face was straight, but his eyes were laughing.

The sixty or more very big canvases that covered the walls were all of female nudes—an overpowering array of buttocks, breasts and thighs that had the throng of first-nighters looking slightly bemused over their champagne and caviare.

Dominic slid his arm possessively through Honor's, and drew her close. 'Shall we do the rounds?' he suggested gently.

She nodded, and let him lead her along the row of paintings. She was wearing the only item in her wardrobe that could really be called a cocktail frock, an off-the-shoulder dress in midnight-blue that looked exquisite on her slender figure. It showed off the youthful grace of her arms and throat, and it clung just enough to emphasise her enviably firm bust and hips. She was aware of appreciative male glances turning her way as they walked forward.

It was even less easy to ignore the amount of female attention Dominic aroused. A lot of the women here tonight seemed to know him, and their progress was continually being halted by people stopping them to make small talk.

It was unashamedly gratifying to know she formed one half of a strikingly handsome couple, especially in this glittering company; and Honor couldn't deny that she felt a fierce pride in being on the arm of Dominic Raven this evening. He was ravishingly attractive, and no amount of personal antagonism towards him could disguise that.

Half an hour later, at the end of the salon, they edged out of the crush, and stood together in front of one of the biggest canvases, mercifully left alone at last.

'He's very good,' Honor had to admit, looking up at the huge canvas, which was one of the very best paintings here. Many of the nudes were in poses so similar as to be almost identical. This figure was reclining, the lines of her body treated in bright, shadowless light, the hard edges almost harsh. 'His draughtsmanship is superb.'

'But without emotion. I doubt whether he truly likes women.'

Surprised, she glanced at Dominic's face. 'Why do you say that?' she asked. 'After all, he's exhibiting several dozen pictures of women here!'

He smiled slightly, his eyes fixed on the canvas. 'He has no feeling for the marvellously varied contours and textures of a woman's body. To him, his model is just a technically interesting arrangement of lines and colours. He conveys no tenderness for his subject, no desire. He's a painter who has no real love for woman's body.'

Honor laughed, but it sounded uncomfortable, even to herself. 'But a painter isn't necessarily a lover, Dominic.'

'The painter who is not a lover has no business to paint,' he retorted, turning to her. 'When he paints a nude, a man should not just paint the shape, the line, the colour tones. He should paint the way he feels when he caresses those thighs, when he kisses those breasts.'

Her face hot with embarrassment, she looked away from his intense eyes, up at the cold, bright colours of the painting in front of them. She was thinking of the way he'd kissed her last night, and she knew he was thinking of that, too. 'Maybe that's just because he doesn't paint any shadows,' she said stiffly, refusing to look at him.

'But women aren't just light,' he said softly. 'They are shadow, too. Shadow softens, flatters, emphasises.'

'It hides the truth!'

'What truth?' he asked mockingly. 'The anatomical truth of lines and wrinkles? Or the profound inner truth of a woman's beauty of spirit?'

'Panovka is a Realist,' she argued. 'Obviously he doesn't believe in shadows or spirits.'

Then he will never be loved by any woman,' Dominic said with a slight smile. 'Harsh light is cruel to a woman—and the older she gets, the crueller light becomes. Panovka needs to understand the necessity of shadow, of mystery. This hard, flat treatment isn't compassionate. I get the feeling that I might as well be looking at the illustrations in a gynaecological textbook.'

'Oh, Dominic,' she had to laugh.

'Moreover,' he went on ruthlessly, 'Panovka's taste in female flesh is execrable.' He turned to glance at the painting on their other side. 'All these heavy haunches and bovine bosoms—the man clearly has a mother-fixation.'

'Dominic,' she hushed him, still smiling, 'people will hear you! Anyway, a lot of women do look like that.'

'Then they should go on a diet,' he retorted wickedly. 'All women should look like you.'

'Like *me*?'

'Indeed.' That smoky gaze had turned to her, studying her from head to foot with the same intentness as he had just been studying Panovka's canvas. 'Your figure comes close to perfection, Honor. Slender, graceful as a dancer, with skin like the finest silk . . .'

The blood rushed to Honor's cheeks. 'You promised,' she rebuked him hotly. 'Art for art's sake!'

'My comments were meant in the artistic sense,' he replied with a wicked grin. 'It's irrelevant, however, because Ivan would never be interested in painting you. He likes the earth-mother type, and you represent something altogether more seductive.'

'I want some champagne.' Before she could turn stiffly away, Dominic laughed softly, and lifted her hand to his warm lips. Her cheeks were still flushed as he kissed her hand in mock apology. That the exchange had been noted by amused eyes around the hall made it all the more acutely discomforting.

At that point, a portly man with over-long grey hair and a beard sailed across to them. If the fingers clutching his drink hadn't been paint-stained, the fact that he was the only sloppily dressed person in the room would have made it easy to deduce that he was the artist.

'Dominic!' he said gaily, almost launching himself at Dominic. 'How wonderful to see you at my little show!'

Skilfully, Dominic turned the attempted embrace into a handshake. 'Good to see you, Ivan. This is Honor O'Hara; Honor, meet Ivan Panovka, doyen of the new Realists.'

'You like my paintings?' he beamed at her, his accent heavy East European.

'Very much,' Honor nodded. 'I think your drawing is wonderfully accurate, and your colours are so translucent and bright. It's one of the most refreshing exhibitions I've seen for years.' The compliment sounded horribly trite to Honor, but the artist seemed to lap it up.

'Thank you,' he smiled largely, tugging at his velvet tie with his free hand, 'thank you indeed!' He waved at the big canvas she and Dominic had just been discussing. 'This one is called "Sheila". The masterpiece of the show, I think.'

'It's by far the best,' Dominic nodded. 'And I like it a great deal. You've certainly changed direction in the past year.'

'Since my marriage to Frieda, my life has opened like a flower, Dominic.' They followed his tender gaze to where a Junoesque woman stood in conversation across the room. The lines of her figure corresponded to the beautiful curves and rounds of the paintings. 'She has opened my eyes to a new reality.'

'So it seems,' Dominic said. 'Would you be interested in a commission, Ivan?' he asked smoothly, and to Honor's horror, his eyes were sparkling mischief directly at her. 'I was thinking of having a portrait painted of Honor—in the same style.'

'Ah.' Panovka tilted his shaggy head to study Honor, who was trying to carry this piece of nonsense off with some shred of dignity. The painter sucked his teeth dubiously. 'I could try, I could try. But—forgive me—the type is not ideal. My genius inclines me towards ...' His hands lovingly described generous curves in the air, and Honor felt laughter bubbling up in her throat at Dominic's expression. 'But if you wish it,' Panovka concluded generously, 'I will certainly try and interpret this particular type for you.'

'No, perhaps you're right,' Dominic said gravely. 'It would be unwise to strain your genius too far out of its natural path.'

'The result could not be guaranteed,' the artist conceded. His small eyes took on an almost sly look as he gestured up at the massive canvas behind them. 'But this painting, now. You like it? What do you say?'

'I do like it,' Dominic nodded. 'How much are you asking for it?'

'Ah, my friend, you are too late,' Panovka said genially, though his eyes were still watching Dominic shrewdly. 'The Kendon Gallery want my "Sheila". A painting of this importance should be in a famous gallery, no?'

'If you say so,' Dominic said easily.

'But for a patron like Dominic Raven, exceptions should be made.' He gave a booming laugh, then leaned forward conspiratorially. 'If you want my "Sheila", I can always give Maxie Kendon another canvas, no?' And without further ado, he named a sum which took Honor's breath away. It wasn't much less than she'd paid for her own flat!

Dominic, however, was unfazed. 'Iniquitous, but I suppose it's worth something like that. Where's your horrible little agent?'

Panovka's bushy eyebrows soared. 'You want it?' This time Dominic could not fend off the bear-hug that the artist threw around him. 'A patron of the gods,' Panovka declared lovingly.

Dominic took out his cheque book without ceremony, as though every eye in the room hadn't just turned their way. Honor's astonishment turned to worldly-wise irony as the gallery manager, Panovka's agent, the statuesque Frieda Panovka, and various hangers-on collected like smiling sharks around them. It was a scene more reminiscent of the Stock Exchange than of the high academic realms of art.

When all the *brouhaha* of paying for the canvas was over, and Dominic was offering her a glass of champagne in the relative privacy of an alcove, she met his eyes with a dry look.

'Hypocrite,' she said softly. 'I wouldn't have believed it if I hadn't seen it with my own eyes.'

'Your own cool green eyes,' he smiled. 'Is it hypocrisy to support the arts? Ivan will sell the whole collection now.'

'You don't give a damn about that picture,' she snorted indignantly. 'You've just condemned it, in my hearing, as soulless and cold. You called it a gynaecological illustration! It's nothing more than an investment to you.'

'A lot of great art is soulless and cold,' he said calmly. 'In fact, I quite like the picture—in a cold, soulless sort of way.' His eyes glinted. 'The fact that it's also, as you so accurately point out, an excellent investment just enhances the aesthetic pleasure of ownership.'

'Next you'll be pushing poor Panovka off a bridge, just to make sure your investment goes up in value.'

'As it happens,' he replied, 'I own four other Panovkas, and I'd like to own more. I'd be quite sorry to see Ivan floating down the Thames.'

'Yeah—you'd be crying all the way to the bank,' Honor snorted.

'Besides, I'd hate to face an enraged Frieda,' he added.

Honor shook her head in disillusionment. 'You really took me in back there, with all that romancing about light and shade and the mystery of womanhood.'

'But I meant every word,' Dominic smiled. 'My heart tells me that Ivan's approach is too cold. My eye tells me that his technique is brilliant.'

'And your head tells you that his value is going to keep rising! You're too sophisticated for me,' Honor said wryly. She sipped her champagne, and grew thoughtful. 'How often do you spend that sort of sum on art?'

'Fairly regularly,' he shrugged. 'And it isn't always with

an eye to investment, either.'

'So you're going to hang "Sheila" in your living-room?' she asked, tilting one delicate eyebrow.

'"Sheila" might be a little overpowering in my living-room,' he conceded, looking across the room at the huge nude. 'I had in mind my boardroom at work.'

'The dizzy realms of high art,' Honor sighed. 'Why not put it straight into a bank vault?'

Dominic smiled, and glanced at his watch. 'It's time I took you home.'

She checked her own watch, and noted that it was almost ten. Time had flown tonight, as it always seemed to do in his company. 'I suppose you had. Before I turn back into Cinderella.'

They said their goodbyes. Panovka had clearly been celebrating with champagne, and was more effusive than ever, but in the end they got away.

In the reserved car park outside, she smiled at him. 'I've enjoyed tonight, Dominic.'

'So have I.' His eyes drifted up and down her figure. 'I don't seem to have had the time to tell you how exquisite you look this evening. That blue sets your colouring off beautifully.'

'It was my mother's favourite colour.' She looked down in confusion. 'She—she wore it on special occasions.'

'Then I'm doubly flattered,' he said softly. 'She must have been a lovely woman.'

'She was,' Honor nodded.

She was subdued on the way home. It had been an odd evening. Apart from one or two clashes, there had been none of the fierce antagonism she'd felt towards Dominic on previous occasions. Instead, a warm, almost intimate feeling had grown up between them, making her all too aware of his ability to bewitch and enchant.

Yet this glimpse of the way Dominic lived had also had its disturbing aspects. Only a very rich man could afford to buy art at that level. The casual way he'd signed away the price of a decent flat for fifteen yards of canvas had flabbergasted her. It was way, way out of her league, beyond her experience.

Why had he asked her to come with him tonight? Because he got a perverse relish out of the company of a woman who was often actively hostile towards him? Or had he wanted to impress her, had she been brought along as an audience for that impressive piece of art-buying?

'You're very sombre,' he commented as they neared the flat.

'I'm just wondering what my role was supposed to be tonight,' she answered him with absolute honesty.

'Your role?' he echoed in amusement. 'You make it sound very complicated. I just wanted to see you. And I want to see you again, soon.'

'I don't think that's a good idea,' Honor said quietly.

He glanced at her. 'Why not?'

'For one thing, it would upset Prudence a great deal.'

'Is that how you intend to live the rest of your life?' he enquired drily. 'Consulting your younger sister about every move?' His voice was velvety. 'Don't you want to see me again—for your own reasons?'

'No,' she said unhappily. 'I think I should steer clear of you, Dominic. You've been bad luck to me so far.'

'Bad luck? What is that?' he snorted. 'Some dark Celtic superstition? You should have left all that behind you in Dublin, in your teens.'

'Besides,' she sighed, 'I'm just not your type.'

'What is my type, then?'

'Someone sophisticated, rich, poised . . . like those women at the gallery tonight.'

'My life is overcrowded with women like that,' he said impatiently. 'They mean nothing to me, Honor. But you—you're special.' He pulled up in the mews, and turned to her intently. 'You distrust me. You probably think you hate me.' His eyes glittered in the darkness. 'Yet my feelings towards you are very, very different, Honor. You can't deny me the chance to show you just how real my feelings are.'

'I need time!' Her heart was pounding now. 'Give me time, Dominic, please! You're crowding me, not giving me chance to collect my wits——'

'You don't need your wits,' he growled. But she caught the gleam of his smile. 'I'll call you at the weekend. Is that long enough?'

'Not really,' she said, shaking her glossy head. But she didn't refuse him. She couldn't. Her own need to see him was already rising at the prospect of their imminent separation.

Nor did she draw back as he leaned across to kiss her on the mouth. His touch was warm, and the memory of last night rose up bright and erotic in her mind. This man had some pagan magic that she would always respond to. Her lips trembled against his, and he laughed softly as he released her. 'Take care,' he murmured. 'You mean a lot to me.'

In the event, it was she who contacted him, not the other way round.

Toby's call came on Thursday morning, at work.

The payphone bleeps sounded for a few seconds, followed by the sound of coins rattling. Then her brother's voice, high-pitched and shaky. 'Honor, it's me, Toby.'

'Toby, what's the matter?' she said urgently.

'The police w-wouldn't let me call you until now.'

'Has something happened to you?' she asked, her heart starting to thud.

'N-no. I mean, yes. I'm at Finsbury Park police station. I've been here all night. I've b-been arrested.'

'Toby!'

'Can you come down?' She knew by his tone of voice that

he was desperate. 'Can you b-bring a lawyer? It's serious this time. I think they're going to charge me today.'

'What for?' she demanded in dread.

'Drugs,' he said painfully.

'What have you *done*?' she yelped in horror.

'I can't say. Not now.'

'I'll be there as soon as I can,' she said tightly, despair haunting her green eyes. She didn't waste time on questions or recriminations. She cut him off, and immediately rang Mark MacDonald's office to ask for the day off. He didn't even ask her what it was about, just told her to take as long as she needed. Then she sat thinking for a moment, that old, sick dread in her stomach. She'd prayed that Toby's follies and adventures would come to an end, soon, but it seemed it was not to be.

She reached for the phone again, and rang Harold Vaughan, their elderly family solicitor.

'Mr Vaughan's on holiday at the moment,' the secretary replied. 'Shall I put you on to Mr Capstaff?'

Honor groaned inwardly. Colin Capstaff was Harold Vaughan's younger partner, a conceited little man who'd once made a determined pass at her. He was hardly suitable, but it looked as though she didn't have much choice. 'Yes, please,' she said.

'Mr Capstaff's line's busy. Will you hold?'

'Yes, I will,' Honor sighed. She leaned back in her chair and closed her eyes. Why was she always doomed to be the one to take responsibility in every crisis? And why did there have to be quite so many crises?

If you ever need any help—with your family, or anything else—will you get in touch with me, first? The deep voice echoed in her mind, and for a moment, she couldn't place the sentence. Then she realised. Her thoughts had turned instinctively, without reason, to Dominic.

He'd offered his help, and she knew he'd meant it. But why on earth should he help her? For that matter, why should she ask him? He already knew a great deal too much about her family.

And yet . . . *Dominic.* So powerful, so capable. Bitter as the choice was, Honor knew that he would probably achieve far more than either Harold Vaughan or the vain Mr Capstaff. But would he? At least she could ask.

Except that would mean putting herself in Dominic Raven's power. Chalking up a debt of gratitude that might cost her very dear indeed. If he did agree to help, it would surely only be to gain possession of some kind over her!

For Toby's sake . . .

She hesitated in momentary anguish over the receiver. How many times in her life had she compromised, gone against her better judgement, involved herself in untold trouble—for Toby's sake? Or if not for him, then for Dad, or for Pru . . .

She couldn't help it. It wasn't in her to refuse to help any of them, not when the trouble was serious and imminent. If Dominic would advise her, no matter out of what motives, his strength and experience would be formidable allies.

The decision was made. She cut the solicitor's office off, and hunted for the Raven Security number.

Dominic was in a meeting, and at first the cool receptionist wouldn't put her through to him. When, with much misgivings, the receptionist gave in to her pleading and connected her, Dominic's deep voice was edged with irritation.

'Honor? What is it?'

She told him, the words spilling over one another. 'You offered to help,' she finished agitatedly. 'I know it's a lot to ask, but I thought you might know someone . . .'

'Who represented your brother last time he was in court?' he asked succinctly.

'A barrister called Lena Tregoran—Toby got her through Legal Aid.'

'I think we can do better,' he said calmly. 'We'd better

get across to Finsbury police station as soon as possible. We'll go in my car. Can you arrange the day off at such short notice?'

'Yes, I've done that already. But Dominic, I'm so——'

'Will you be waiting outside your office in thirty minutes?'

'Yes,' she said breathlessly. And before she could thank him, he'd hung up.

Instinctively, she knew that she'd made the right decision—from Toby's point of view, anyway. There was a purposeful intentness about Dominic that had given her something to hope for already.

It was tempting to leave Pru in blissful ignorance for the time being, given her upset state, but Honor knew she'd better say something. She rang Pru at home, and broke the news to her as gently as she could.

'Not again,' Pru wailed. 'What's he been up to *this* time?'

'I don't quite know yet. I'm going to the station right away to see what I can do.'

'I'll come with you.'

'You can't,' Honor said hastily, thinking of what Pru would say when she knew she'd asked Dominic Raven to help.

'Why not?' Pru wanted to know.

'I don't want you upset any further,' Honor said truthfully. 'Besides, someone from work's giving me a lift right now. I'll see you tonight, love. You just relax.'

'Well, if you're sure——' Pru said, plainly not all that keen to go anyway.

'I'm sure,' Honor said firmly.

Dominic wasn't even a minute late. She felt her unhappy heart lift as the black Porsche rumbled up to the kerb, exactly half an hour later. Just the thought of his calm strength was enough to stop the nerves from jumping in her stomach. Thank God he'd come! She was trying to thank him as she climbed in beside him, but he didn't seem to be interested.

'This is the fourth time he's been arrested?' he asked grimly. She nodded, anxiously watching his profile as he accelerated through the traffic. 'Did he tell you what he was going to be charged with, exactly?'

'He just said drugs. Oh, Dominic . . . I'm so very sorry to drag you into this. Have you left an important meeting for me?'

'Nothing that won't wait.' The light cream suit he wore emphasised his dark colouring and superb build; yet the stunning glamour of his good looks was undercut by the grim expression on his face. 'Your brother has a talent for disaster, it seems.'

Timidly, she laid her hand on his arm, aware of the hard muscle beneath the fine cloth. 'I'm very grateful . . .'

He didn't respond to the gesture. 'I've contacted the best lawyer I know in London. He's busy right now, but he'll get to your brother as soon as he can.' He glanced at her, black eyes intent. 'This could be bad for him, Honor. He's got beyond the stage of second chances and suspended sentences.'

'I know,' she said in a thin voice.

'Tell me about him,' he commanded.

She did her best to give him some idea of Toby's character and problems, and he listened in silence, only asking questions when she ran out of words. 'He's *not* wicked,' she told Dominic urgently. 'He's just never had a proper chance. Maybe if he'd managed to get a decent job, things would have been very different. He's so talented, Dominic . . .'

Dominic drove fast and confidently as she talked, using the car's power to take advantage of every gap in the traffic. It was she who did most of the talking during the fast drive, trying to turn his disapproval into compassion. But he didn't say anything more until they were walking up to the charge desk at Finsbury Park police station.

'If you love your brother,' he told her shortly, 'don't interfere. Understood?'

'Understood,' she nodded. She was almost unaware of the fact that she was clinging to his arm, pressing her body against the protective strength of his presence, as he introduced her to the desk sergeant and explained why they were there.

'The arresting officer's not here at the moment, sir,' he said in answer to Dominic's question. 'That's PC Harris. He comes on duty this evening.'

Dominic nodded. 'Is there any chance that Toby will be released?' Dominic asked quietly.

'That depends on the evidence, I'm afraid.' The sergeant glanced in a register. 'There are still some reports to come in this morning.'

'Forensic reports?' Dominic asked. The policeman nodded. He had a pleasant, weary face, a pleasant, weary voice.

'Shouldn't be too long before we get the results back, sir,' he said consolingly.

'And the likelihood of a criminal charge?'

'Not my department, sir,' the sergeant said stolidly. 'It's up to my chief. I should say it's probable.'

'When?'

'Probably tomorrow.'

'Sure?' Dominic queried.

'Sure as I can be.'

'I see,' Dominic nodded. 'Can we speak to him, please?'

'I'll have him brought through.'

The interview room was grey and windowless, and a bored-looking WPC was on duty there, staring patiently ahead of her.

When Toby was brought in, he was scruffy and unwashed, and his overlong hair didn't improve the picture. He looked awful. She glanced with quick shame at Dominic to see his reaction to her brother, but his face remained expressionless.

'Toby,' she said quietly, 'this is Dominic Raven. He's a friend.'

'Hi.' Toby's green eyes, like Honor's but paler and smaller, flicked unhappily between the two of them. 'Did you bring a lawyer?'

'I've arranged for David Callaghan to come and see you,' Dominic said quietly. 'He's good. He'll come some time today. But you're likely to be in here for another day or two, at least. I presume you need clothes?'

'Yeah, I do.' Toby ran his hands through his tousled black hair, his thin face pale and unhappy. His skin was glistening with sweat, and he looked ill. 'I could do with all sorts of things.' Toby's Irish accent was far more noticeable than Honor's, but his voice was somehow younger than hers.

'Have you made a statement yet?' Dominic asked.

Toby shook his head with a lop-sided smile. 'I'm not that stupid.'

'Of course not,' Dominic said silkily. 'You're an old hand at this game, aren't you, Toby?'

Something in the tone of his voice wiped the smile off Toby's face. 'They picked me up late last night.' He fumbled in the pocket of his denim shirt for a cigarette. 'I had some coke, just a tiny bit that someone had given me. It's—it's not really my scene, so I sold it to this feller from Muswell Hill. That's when they jumped us.'

'"Coke"?' Honor asked in puzzlement.

'Cocaine,' Dominic translated expressionlessly.

'Oh, Toby!' she said in horror.

'How much did you sell?' Dominic asked, his mouth a harsh line.

'I don't know.' Toby hung his head miserably. 'A little tiny bit. Just a few quid's worth.' He was twenty-six, and he looked sixteen. A very frightened sixteen.

Dominic's fingers were drumming a devil's tattoo on the table. 'They arrested you both?'

'Yeah.'

'Where did you get it from?'

'A—a feller gave it to me,' Toby stammered.

'A—a feller gave it to you,' Dominic mimicked him cruelly. 'Do you think I'm a bloody fool?'

'N-no,' Toby said, blinking at Dominic's harsh reaction. 'No, I remember now, I bought it.'

'From a dealer?' Toby's wide mouth quivered slightly before he nodded. Dominic grunted. 'How much are you using, Toby?'

'I told you,' Toby said, eyes twisting away from Dominic's, 'coke just isn't my scene. That's why I s-sold that stuff in the first place. I don't use it, and that's God's truth.'

'How much are you using?' Dominic repeated with a rasp in his voice.

'I'm a wine and whisky man, Mr Raven——'

'Come on, Honor.' Dominic was already on his feet, hauling Honor up with effortless strength. 'Let's go.'

'But what's going to happen to him?' she asked Dominic in dread.

'He's going to go to jail,' Dominic said calmly. 'It's by far the best place for him.'

Toby's face went paler still, and Honor felt tears swelling under her lid.

'I thought you said he was a *friend*?' Toby whimpered accusingly.

'That was cruel,' Honor said in a low voice to Dominic, holding his gaze with darkened green eyes. 'Did you have to say that?'

'It's the truth.' Dominic glanced at the wretched figure of Toby with complete indifference. 'He's a liar and a thief already, and he's well on the way to becoming a hopeless junkie.'

'Dominic, no!' she gasped in shock at the careless brutality of his words.

Toby stubbed out his cigarette with shaking fingers. 'All right,' he said unsteadily. 'I've smoked it a couple of times. But I'm not an addict.' He looked up pleadingly, not at his sister, but at Dominic. 'I'm sorry I lied to you. I—I didn't want Honor to know . . .'

'It's about time she knew,' Dominic said curtly. He sat down again, much to Toby's obvious relief, and Honor sank down beside him, her legs feeling like jelly. 'How old is your friend?' Dominic asked, ignoring her now.

'I dunno,' Toby said hopelessly. 'Maybe a few years younger than me.'

'Not a kid?'

Toby sat up indignantly. 'What do you think I am?'

'An idiot,' Dominic told him succinctly. 'How often were you smoking the stuff?'

'Every couple of days.' His eyes drifted to Honor's appalled face, then flicked away again. 'Nothing serious.'

'Nothing serious,' Dominic repeated. His voice still held that dangerous rasp. 'I would have thought that having observed your own father's alcoholism from close-up might have given you some insight into what was "serious" and what was not.'

Honor couldn't help wincing. Toby was almost on the verge of tears. This was a nightmare. It couldn't be happening. 'Is he really going to prison?' she asked Dominic.

'Considering the fact that he's been convicted three times already,' Dominic said cooly, 'and assuming that his friend from Muswell Hill gives evidence against him—which he almost certainly will—yes, Toby will go to prison.'

'Please,' Toby said in a low voice, 'can you help me? I swear to God I'll never do it again. I'll never touch the evil stuff. Just get me out of here.'

'What on earth do you imagine I can do?' Dominic asked, arching one disdainful eyebrow.

'You know the score,' Toby nodded, twisting his hands

together. 'You could do something.' Strange, Honor thought absently, how rapidly people recognised the authority in Dominic. It occurred to her that his life must be filled with weak people demanding his help. 'I couldn't go to jail,' Toby whimpered. 'I'd die. Look, Mr Raven, I mean it. I'll never touch any drugs again in my life. *Please.*'

Dominic considered Toby with brooding eyes. 'If I did agree to help you—and I haven't said I will—it would be on one conditon.'

'Anything,' Toby said, nodding his tousled head vigorously. 'What?'

'That you do *exactly* what I tell you.' Dominic's tone was uncompromising, and Toby's eyes held a glimmer of hope for the first time.

'I will, I swear it.'

'I'll be in touch.' Honor felt the pressure of his fingers around her arm, and for the second time that morning, rose to stand beside him.

Toby rubbed his face in his hands, then looked up at them with bleary eyes. 'Thanks. I will do anything you ask, I promise. And I'm sorry, Honor. I really am.'

She kissed his cheek, trying not to let the threatening tears intervene, and followed Dominic out of the police station.

'There's not much we can do here,' he told her outside. 'It's up to the prosecutor to decide whether or not he's going to be charged. But there are various ways and means of averting the worst. I'm going to have to make a call to a friend, Honor. Someone who might help. You wait in the car.'

She took the keys from him, and sat in the Porsche while Dominic went to the payphone across the street. Through the tinted glass of the booth his tall figure seemed dark, mysterious. Would he really be able to do anything for Toby? What a mess! When in God's name was Toby ever going to grow up?

Dominic got back into the car. 'I've just spoken to a good friend of mine, called Helen Matthews. We're meeting her around four this afternoon,' he said, and smiled slightly. 'I think you'll find her interesting. She's an extraordinarily persuasive woman. If she'd been born poor, she'd have ended up a millionaire by thirty.' He gave her a dry smile. 'As it is, she was born very rich, so she divides her talents between ten or a dozen different committees of varying importance and influence.'

'What sort of committees?'

'The one that concerns us is the Police Drugs Liaison Committee. She chairs that one. If she backs us up, I'm fairly sure we can persuade the public prosecutor to let Toby have another chance. As long as Toby will play ball.' His eyes were enigmatic. 'Do you think you can persuade *her* that Toby's a worthwhile cause?'

'I don't know,' Honor said nervously. Ms Matthews sounded a rather formidable lady. 'He really isn't a bad person—just wild. Prison would kill him. He's too sensitive to survive something like that. Do you really think you can help?' she pleaded. 'I'd give anything.'

'Would you indeed?' he asked, arching one eyebrow wickedly.

'Almost anything,' she said, colouring. 'I know you must despise him . . .'

'No,' Dominic replied calmly, 'I don't despise him. He seems a nice kid.'

'"A nice kid"?' she echoed in astonishment. 'You treated him like scum in there!'

'Did you expect me to pat him on the head and tell him he'd been a good boy?' Dominic's lip curled. 'He's been a complete fool, and he badly needs to be told it. If he gets away without a sentence, the fright may well have done him a great deal of good. But I agree with you that prison would be a disaster for him.'

'Dominic, I had no idea he was using cocaine.' She

glanced at his tanned face with unhappy eyes. 'That gave me a horrible shock. I feel so *guilty* . . .'

'For not looking after your twenty-six-year-old brother?' Dominic retorted. 'Don't be ridiculous. He's old enough to know that drugs can kill.'

'But I should have known. I would have been able to talk to him . . .'

'He needs more than talking to,' Dominic said decisively. 'He needs a completely radical change of life-style.'

'Is he—is he an addict?' she ventured.

'He looked as though he was going through minor withdrawal symptoms.' Dominic glanced in the rearview mirror before pulling out and into the traffic. 'Cocaine isn't as addictive as other drugs, but it usually leads on to serious trouble. But no, I don't think he's an addict. I think he's an overgrown kid who spends most of his time either feeling sorry for himself, or looking for illicit kicks.'

Honor nodded slowly. Now that the initial panic was receding, she was just starting to appreciate her own temerity in asking Dominic for help. Given her earlier feelings towards the big man, it hadn't exactly been in character, had it? Yet he'd come, instantly and without question. Moreover, she trusted implictly that he would do much to help her errant brother.

And this was the man she'd so recently judged cold, destructive, arrogant, utterly hateful . . .

'That's a fair assessment of Toby's character,' she couldn't help smiling, 'You're very perceptive.'

'Am I?' He turned an ironical glance her way. 'Then why can't I figure you out?'

'Me?' Honor felt her expression grow embarrassed. 'You can't possibly find me hard to understand!'

'On the contrary,' he drawled, 'I find you exceptionally hard to understand. For one thing, how did you turn out so sane while the rest of your family is so crazy? For another, being so sane, how can you be so full of prejudices about me? And for a third, how did you manage to get me away from an important board meeting this morning to go chasing around the police stations of North London?'

'I'm sorry about your board meeting,' she said awkwardly. 'And I think I'm beginning to lose some of my prejudices about you. You've been marvellous this morning.' Her cheeks flushed at the topic she was about to bring up. 'Dominic, I—I want to say something. about the way I've been behaving towards you,' she said hesitantly. 'It's all been a bit of a mess, I'm afraid.'

'"All"?' he queried gently.

'I've said a lot of things I shouldn't have said. I wish you could understand that it was just my pain for Pru spilling over into anger. You see, Pru has very strong feelings against you, which is understandable. Isn't it?' He didn't answer her question, so she went on, 'Anyway, I think—I think I've been a lot more aggressive than I needed to be ...'

'Why not put all that behind us?' he suggested gently. 'And start all over again?'

'I'd like that,' Honor said in a small voice. 'You frighten me sometimes, Dominic. I don't quite know how to react to you ...'

'You're not exactly approachable yourself,' he smiled. 'Mature beyond your years, green eyes. You give off some very cool and poised vibrations, especially when your back's up.' He gave her a glinting look from the tails of his eyes. 'Which is why it's a revelation to see you in a crisis like this one.'

'I'm afraid my pose tends to slip slightly,' she laughed with a release of tension.

'It certainly reveals more about your true character,' he agreed casually.

'Oh? In what way?'

'It's easy to see how much you care, for one thing. You're obviously a woman with deep, strong feelings, deeply feminine and loving.'

Her cheeks hot, Honor stared straight ahead in silence. The conversation had suddenly grown very personal, and she wasn't sure how to take that; why was she so susceptible to Dominic when she'd decided so firmly that he was going to mean nothing to her?

'Where are we going now?' she asked.

'Something to eat, first of all. And then we've got a couple of hours to while away. Have you ever been to Kew Gardens?'

'Not since I was a girl,' she smiled.

'Good,' he nodded. 'Since we're playing truant together, we might as well enjoy ourselves. Besides, I think you need something to take your mind off your family for a couple of hours. I know two good restaurants near here. You decide—French or Italian?'

CHAPTER FIVE

An hour later, after a light lunch, they pulled up outside the main entrance of Kew. He'd been so kind and attentive over the meal that her heart had almost completely melted towards him.

'I'm so grateful, Dominic,' she began, turning to him, but he laid a finger on her lips.

'I haven't done anything yet. It remains to be see whether we manage to get Toby out of this mess.'

'Thank you, anyway.' Impulsively, she leaned forward, and kissed him lightly on the mouth. His eyes glinted dangerously.

'Is that my reward?' He pulled her close with easy strength, and kissed her back. But this time the kiss deepend into passion. Her lips parted moistly, inviting his tongue to slide into her mouth, teasing her with wicked expertise. Her heart was pounding as she touched his tongue timidly with her own, feeling her own response racing along her veins as he held her close to him. After the tension of the morning, this excitement was like speed: it robbed you of breath, made your senses swim . . .

It was a long, intoxicatingly deep kiss, and when at last he released her, her head was spinning as though she'd drunk too much wine.

His mouth caressed her temples hungrily, inhaling her perfume as though he were aching for her every bit as much as she was aching for him. '*That* was more like a reward. Now let's go, before I eat you alive.'

She climbed out of the car with shaky legs.

'And stop worrying,' he commanded, dark eyes smiling at her expression.

The wind fluttered her airy linen skirt, bringing a cool touch of relief in a day that was almost too hot for comfort. 'Somehow I'd never imagined you as a lover of flowers,' she said.

'Oh, I'm a determined gardener. Besides,' he added silkily, 'flowers are noted for their effect on female resistance.'

Beyond the high wall, the fairytale grandeur of the great garden baked in the sun. Determined to simply enjoy the glory of the moment, Honor pulled her rich black hair away from her face, and felt the tension ebb out of her muscles.

'How is Prudence?' Dominic asked casually, the question intruding into her happy trance with an unwelcome reality.

'It's hard to say,' she sighed. 'I suppose the first shock is over by now, but she's far from getting over it. I don't know whether she ever will get over it.'

'Isn't that a little dramatic?' he asked coolly.

The edge of irony in his tone made her frown.

'You're so certain that Pru's feelings are shallow,' she retorted. What makes you so hard on her? Could you really have seen into her heart on the strength of a few casual meetings?'

'Perhaps not,' he agreed, without any sign of repentance. 'But Prudence is only nineteen. It's not uncommon for the emotions of nineteen to come and go very quickly, and to mean little.'

'I can see it's a long time since *you* were nineteen,' Honor said. She accompanied the remark with a half-smile, but she meant it as a rebuke, none the less, and he nodded.

'*Touché*. Maybe I'm too cynical, after all.'

'In Pru's case, I think you are. She loves Mog very deeply.' Honor glanced at him. 'I have to admit I had my own suspicions about Pru's feelings towards Mog.'

'Indeed?' He gave her a dry look, and she had to laugh.

'OK,' she admitted, 'maybe your judgement wasn't *that* unreasonable. But the way Pru's been since Mog left for America proves one thing—she cared for him very deeply, and she's been badly hurt by what happened.'

Dominic took her arm, but was silent as they walked. After a few minutes, he said, almost inconsequentially, 'Your sister is a very pretty girl. And like most pretty girls of nineteen, she's both frivolous and flirtatious. It's not always easy to credit her with deep feelings.' There was nothing in the smooth, deep voice to indicate any irony, and she had to gnaw her lip in silence. Long brown fingers reached out to brush away the lock of black hair that had fallen over her left eye. 'Are you sure she really loves the boy?'

'He's not a boy, Dominic. He's a man. And she's a grown woman.' Now she was all too aware of the muscular body beside hers, of the way her breast brushed against his arm as they walked. The truce they'd agreed on so recently was proving a lot more fragile—and difficult to sustain—than she'd anticipated. 'Let's drop it—I don't want to argue,' she pleaded.

'Nor do I. I just wonder what *love* is, sometimes.' Dark eyes mocked her with a hidden smile. 'There are many other feelings that might draw two people together.'

'Such as?' she challenged.

'Such as sex, for example,' he said. 'Such as one of the people being extremely wealthy, and the other rather poor.'

'How can you be so cynical?' she accused. When he attacked Pru, all her confusion was suddenly resolved. She knew exactly where her loyalities lay. 'I realise that your work brings you up against a lot of mean, crooked little people, but my sister isn't one of them. You haven't any right to say such disparaging things about her.'

'Well now,' he said gently, 'we seem to have a difference of opinion. You think I'm too cynical. And I think you're being deliberately naïve.'

'I know my sister!' She was upset enough to want to pull away from him, but his fingers were like steel, stopping her. 'She's not just out for money, and she's not just out for sex. You obviously don't understand the first thing about Prudence, or you wouldn't imply such horrible things!'

'Sex isn't horrible,' he said with a smile.

'It is—if it isn't accompanied by love,' she told him firmly.

'In which case,' he asked in a tone of velvety smoothness, 'would you kindly explain what happened between you and me the other night? Was that pure, horrible sex—or was it love?'

Her cheeks flamed in confusion. 'I think—well, obviously that was just sex.'

'Obviously?' he said, one eyebrow tilting. 'Just sex? Then I take it you despise yourself for the way you reacted?'

'Sex and love are very different things, Dominic.' She heard the spinsterish meanness in her own voice, and hated herself for it. She tried to sound more adult. 'What happened was a physical thing. It doesn't imply any deeper feelings.'

'Doesn't it?' He was cool now, his slightly mocking smile rebuking her words. 'Don't blush, Honor. I was asking what seemed to me a perfectly natural question—given the circumstances.'

'There *are* no circumstances,' she said determinedly. They were approaching the Temperate House by now, a vast and glittering cathedral of glass covering well over half an acre, but she was hardly aware of her surroundings any more.

'I have to grant you courage,' he drawled. 'Given the fact that your errant brother will almost certainly be prosecuted unless I can help him, it might seem logical for you to be rather more—amiable.'

'You're too much of a gentleman to take advantage of a woman in my position,' she snapped icily.

'Let me tell you two certain facts.' He pulled her round to face him, and the impact of his deep eyes was piercing. 'Firstly, I'm no gentleman, Honor. And secondly, I'm not doing this out of altruistic regard for Toby. I'm doing it for *you.*' He held her gaze for a moment longer, then led her into the vast greenhouse. 'Look at that,' he remarked easily, staring upwards. 'And they say Victorian architects were uninspired.'

She was too upset to do more than glance upwards. The tracery of the huge roof hung high above them, like a gigantic cobweb against the blue sky. 'Very nice,' she said, tight-lipped. What did he want of her? Humility, an agreement with everything he said about Pru? By calling Pru names, he was only hardening her loyalty. Nothing was surer to bring out her claws than to hear Pru being attacked by this big, confident tiger of a man.

Or, much more disturbingly, was he expecting her to reward his help with her body? Sleep with him in exchange for Toby's release?

'This is one of the great plant collections of the world,' Dominic said, apparently completely unaffected by her tense silence. Some of the most beautiful rhododendrons and azaleas of all are grown here.' He strolled ahead of her, clearly enjoying himself. Reluctantly, Honor tried to swallow her anger, and cast a perfunctory glance at the strange beauties all around them.

It *was* a marvellous piece of gardening. The subtropically moist air was heady, and despite the cold spring weather outside, many rhododendrons were blooming exquisitely. The variety of form and colour in the beds was bewildering. The most vivid blooms caught the eye first, whites splashed with reds and purples and yellows; yet the more modest ones could be just as beautiful. Pale greens and creams and pinks blended in delicate harmony. It was a vast, exotic world, unlike any greenhouse she'd ever seen.

'I didn't expect to see flowers at this time of year,' she said briefly.

'Most of these plants come from the Himalayas and the mountains of South-East Asia,' Dominic informed her, watching the anger fading out of her face. He leaned against the railing, folding his arms. 'They flower very early, especially under glass.'

'They're exquisite,' she said, approaching a low-growing shrub. 'And this one's scented!' she exclaimed. 'The only rhododendrons I knew were those purple ones you see in the woods.'

'There are a lot more varieties than that one,' he smiled. He came over to her, tilting her chin up so that he could look down into her face. 'Ah,' he smiled, 'those beautiful green eyes are clear again. They go quite dark when you're angry, like the sea in foul weather.' He kissed the tip of her nose with wicked amusement. 'Irish eyes look best smiling. Let's walk.'

She let him lead her along the paths between the plant-beds, listening to him. It was obvious that his knowledge of plants ran deep. He spoke with confidence and authority, and she found herself fascinated by the strange, sometimes bizarre species that grew in this amazing palace of glass. And a little understanding made the plants themselves all the more beautiful. They were exotic things, as unlike domestic English flowers as Dominic himself was different from most men. Her feelings about him were like a yo-yo!

He led her up the spiral iron staircase to the gallery high above. Here, just beneath the glass roof, they were utterly alone, the solitude and peace vast all around the warm, secure haven of this greenhouse. She was totally wrapped up in what he was saying as she stared downwards at the jungle-world spread below, her lips parted. The touch of his fingers against her cheek was startling, making her flinch, her eyes widening as she found herself looking up into dark eyes that brimmed with amusement.

'You look so beautiful,' he said apologetically. 'Like a Pre-Raphaelite painting.'

She tried to smile it off, but she could see the laughter in his eyes turning to something else. 'You don't really want to hear any more about the sex-life of plants, do you?' he asked softly. She shook her head. The skin of her face had taken on a moist glow, her eyelids drugged by the warm, humid atmosphere of the Temperate House. When he drew her against his hard body, she didn't resist, raising her mouth to his kiss again with a dizzy renewal of hunger. With unsteady fingers, she caressed his thick, crisp hair, her fingertips trailing down his hard cheek, tracing the muscular line of his neck.

There was something new this morning, an intimacy that hadn't been there before she'd asked him for help. His tongue ran smoothly between her lips, plunging deeper into her mouth as his thighs tautened against hers, the thrust of his body unambiguously demanding.

'You're so desirable,' he groaned, his mouth travelling across her throat. Honor arched her neck back, intoxicated by his desire. As if he understood her wishes before they were even expressed, she felt his sharp teeth bite her throat, hungry as a wolf for her woman's body.

'Dominic,' she whispered shakily, 'I prayed you'd never do this to me again . . .'

'And now?' he asked with a soft laugh. His hands were beneath her flimsy blouse, roaming across the sculpted slenderness of her back. 'Now you know you want me,' he said with velvety authority. 'As much as I want you.'

His teeth grazed the soft skin of her shoulder as he inhaled the perfume of her body. Then his hands had moved to the silk-cupped curves of her breasts, caressing their fullness in his palms. The ache that had been in them all week was instantly gone, the tender pink tips hardening in excitement through the sheer silk of her bra. She dug her fingernails into the hard muscles of his back, her hands claiming his body with possessive urgency as their mouths met.

Honor gasped as his thumbs moved with slow appreciation across her nipples, the sensation at first electric, then changing to a languorous warmth that invaded her thighs, spreading an exqusite need through the womb of her body. She was giddily aware of the thrust of his hips against her, instinctively knowing how he ached to fill her with the hard, hot arousal she could feel in his loins.

The knowledge seemed to melt her inside, her womanhood instantly honeyed with the moistness that would allow him to thrust firmly, deeply, into her . . .

Voices intruded into the ecstasy of the moment as a party of tourists began filing into the Temperate House below them.

'Damn,' he said softly, but with feeling. Passion had made him even more devastatingly handsome, the colour vivid in his high cheekbones. 'We'd better go.'

Honor pulled away shakily, her hands barely in control as she straightened her blouse, the silk brushing with unbearable tension against her full breasts.

They walked down the stairway and out into the air, both of them tense and silent. Heavy clouds had covered the sun in the time they'd been in the Temperate House, and the breeze was cold on her sensitive skin after the sub-tropical humidity they'd just been in. She shivered miserably, her clothes feeling too thin for comfort. Without a word, Dominic pulled of his jacket, and draped it around her slender shoulders. She hugged the warmth of it around her. It smelled of him, of his body, his aftershave.

It had happened again, exactly as she had sworn it never would. With an ease that made her defences look ridiculous, he'd taken control of her. Toby was sitting in prison, and she'd melted into his arms, every other thought driven from her head by the pressure of his lips, the caress of his hands.

Was *this* why she'd asked him to help Toby? Not because she thought he could really help, but because deep down inside he was coming to dominate her thoughts?

The realisation of her own deepening feelings came as a shock. She'd been very blind about Dominic up to now. But she could hardly fool herself—or him—for much longer.

Nothing in her life seemed to take as long as the ten-minute walk back to the car. He opened the door for her, then walked round to ease his lithe body behind the wheel. But before he switched on the ignition, he turned to her. 'By your heavy silence,' he said gently, 'I assume you're consumed with guilt again?'

'Not exactly,' she replied in a low voice.

'You're certainly not pleased with yourself,' he said drily, then smiled slightly. 'Your mouth tells me you've kissed other men before. You're no innocent, green eyes. So why this tension about sex? Is it just me? Or do you still blame me for what happened to Prudence?'

She didn't answer. She could hardly tell him that her

heavy silence stemmed from her realisation that she was, irrevocably, falling under his spell!

Dominic stared at her downcast face for a moment longer, then shrugged, and started the car. 'We'd better get over to Helen's house,' he said briefly.

Honor clipped the safety-belt round her. It was hardly a satisfactory conclusion to those fiery moments of passion in the Temperate House.

She felt a sudden flush of shame. Dominic was giving her so much, and all she could do was curl up defensively, like a hedgehog. How timid, how ungenerous!

Yet she couldn't help the way she was. Her emotions ran very deep, that was her nature. Love would not be a fleeting thrill, she knew that fully; it would be a profound, immensely powerful emotion, against which she would have no real defences.

And while her emotion developed in her, like life in a mother's womb, it was her instinct to hug it in silence.

Irrational, yes, but it was the way Honor was made. She could not share this burgeoning feeling with anyone, not yet—not even with the man who had caused it to grow. She had to wrap herself around the growing passion in her heart, perhaps just for a few more days.

She glanced at Dominic's intent profile. No feeling of loyalty to Pru's feelings would stop her from answering his passion, when she was ready. And as for sex—it was true that she was not a virgin. Nor, on the other hand, was she very experienced. Prudence, who was six years younger than her, had infinitely more experience with men than she had. She knew that Pru had had several lovers since she was seventeen.

But Pru's nature was warmer than hers, her sexuality less hidden. Since her early teens, Honor had been forced to be an adult, caring for Pru, trying to care for Toby and Dad, too. She'd hardly had the time for sex ... except once.

His name had been Peter. He had made love to her one summer, a long time ago, and she'd never seen him since.

It had been a pleasant, though hardly earth-shattering experience. Whatever she'd been expecting—a cosmic upheaval, probably—hadn't materialised. It certainly hadn't matched the mystical delights that D H Lawrence had led her to anticipate!

Reflecting on the loss of her virginity, at twenty, to a man whose face she couldn't quite remember, brought a wry smile to Honor's lips. The clinical details of that lovemaking still amused her. Peter had been a gentle, rather sweet man she'd met at a party, and she'd been an inquisitive lady just out of her teens. And the back of a Renault would have presented problems for the most experienced of lovers ...

'What are you smiling at?' Dominic asked gently. She glanced at him, green eyes warm.

'Just something silly that once happened to me. I'm sorry if I seemed sulky just now. And if you think I don't enjoy being kissed by you, then you're being a lot more insecure than you ought to be.'

He arched an eyebrow, then grinned, showing those beautiful white teeth. 'Am I indeed?'

For the rest of the journey, Honor stared out of the window with unseeing eyes, allowing herself to reflect just how close to a cosmic upheaval Dominic's lovemaking could be!

'I understand your concern.'

Helen Matthews was beautiful in an olive-skinned, almost Mediterranean way, and although she wore no jewellery, her predominantly black clothes were very elegant, and—Honor felt—certainly very expensive. She was studying Honor with frank interest. 'Dominic tells me this isn't the first time he's been arrested by the police?'

'No, it isn't. He was charged with possession of cannabis once before, but he was acquitted.' With a distinct sense of embarrassment, Honor added, 'He's also been convicted on two counts of theft.'

'I see.' Helen crossed long, slim legs. 'Has he ever been seen by a psychiatrist?'

'He's just irresponsible,' Honor said in surprise. 'He's not deranged.'

'Helen's simply trying to find something to help mollify the police,' Dominic said gently. He was sitting beside Honor. His arm was stretched casually along the back of the sofa, beind her; and she was grateful for the supportive gesture. There was something about Helen Matthews' assuredness, lover of humanity though she might be, that slightly intimidated Honor. 'Has he ever been seen by a social worker, for example?' Dominic suggested.

'Yes, once or twice, in Islington,' Honor remembered. 'That was some time after our mother died.'

'You don't remember the social worker's name?' Helen asked.

'She was called Mrs Thomas. Elizabeth Thomas.'

'Good.' Helen had taken out a crocodile-skin-bound notebook, and was making quick notes. 'How old was Toby when your mother died?'

'Fifteen.'

There were a lot more questions, and she answered them as honestly as she could—even the questions about her father's drinking, and the spells he'd had in Rosslands.

Helen Matthews was efficient to her fingertips, that was obvious. The almond eyes which were studying Honor so frankly the whole time were brightly intelligent. It would be too easy to dismiss this woman as a rich dilettante; she was obviously a lot more than that.

The room they were sitting in was exquisitely furnished and through the row of high Georgian windows, a beautiful garden was in full bloom. At the back of her mind, she couldn't help wondering about Dominic's relationship with this woman. Had they been lovers? Were they lovers now? A stab of acute jealousy pierced her heart. It was such an alien feeling to Honor that at first she didn't know what it was.

Helen eventually put her notebook away, and uncrossed those elegant legs. 'I think we can work something out between us,' she nodded to Dominic. 'It certainly sounds as though prison isn't the answer.'

'Prison would kill Toby,' Honor said anxiously. 'It would destroy him.'

'It sounds as though he needs something, though,' Helen said thoughtfully. 'It's not unusual for boys to run a little wild after the death of a parent in their teens. But Toby's had eleven years to settle down. How long has he been unemployed?'

'For eighteen months, this time. He's never been out of work that long before.' She couldn't help that flicker of self-blame again. 'I suppose I wasn't aware how much he was suffering. I should have foreseen this . . .'

'Honor has deep-seated guilt feelings about her family,' Dominic said drily. 'She blames herself for their problems.' Helen's bright eyes didn't miss the fact that Dominic's hand brushed Honor's hair gently as he said the words.

'Is your brother a good carpenter?' she asked, offering Honor a cigarette.

'When he gets down to a job, yes, he is,' Honor nodded. 'No thanks, I don't smoke. He's capable of beautiful work. He did my kitchen for me, all the cupboards and worktops, and he's done a professional job.' She shrugged painfully.

'It's just that work is so uncertain in London. He never seems to get anything except short-term jobs.'

'Hmmm.' A thin gold lighter chirruped in Helen's fingers as she lit her cigarette. She exhaled pensively. 'It's a familiar story.'

'He'll pull through,' Honor said with an attempt at a smile.

Dominic shook his head, his expression grim. 'He's fallen in with bad company, Honor. Whatever they say, you don't buy cocaine behind the bike sheds. Helen will tell you that. And if he's been peddling the stuff, even a couple of times, it means he's getting in deep.'

'Yes,' Honor said quietly. 'The same thoughts have been in my mind.'

'He needs a break from London,' Helen said. The clever almond eyes met hers. 'You're obviously a loving sister to him; but you keep pulling him out of the nasty situations he gets himself into, and I don't think that's altogether a good thing. He's been indulged far too long.'

Honor looked away, accepting this new source of blame unhappily. 'Perhaps you're right,' she said awkwardly.

'I agree,' Dominic said decisively. 'Toby needs to go a long way away, preferably to a steady job somewhere.' His eyes probed hers. 'You agree with that assessment?'

'It sounds perfect. But where?' Honor asked unhappily.

'We'll think of something,' Dominic smiled. 'D'you mind if I make some phone calls, Helen? I left things in rather a mess this morning.'

'Use the little study,' Helen nodded, and watched him walk out thoughtfully.

'Do you think there's a hope for him?' Honor asked Helen with worried eyes.

'In the short term, yes. But after this—that's another matter. Have you considered that if he intervenes successfully, Dominic will be tacitly taking responsibility for your brother's future good behaviour?'

'But how can he do that?' Honor asked.

'You tell me.' Helen Matthews leaned back, studying Honor through a curl of cigarette smoke. 'You think Dominic's rather wonderful, don't you?'

Honor was taken aback. 'He's—he's very effective,' she stammered.

'He is, rather,' Helen agreed drily. 'Where did you meet Dominic?'

'Er—at ComTech,' Honor said, not wanting to go into any other details. 'I work there, and Dominic has been advising my boss on security.'

'I see.' Helen tapped ash into the midnight-blue Murano ashtray. 'He seems very fond of you.'

'He's been extremely kind to me,' Honor said uneasily. 'I suppose he feels involved because I turned to him for help. But I don't think it goes any further than that.'

'Don't you?' The leaf-shaped mouth smiled slightly sceptically.

'I really didn't have a right to ask him for help at all,' Honor went on. 'He just seemed so competent, so strong—and I had no one else to turn to. I realise you're only helping Toby because of Dominic, Helen. I'm very grateful, though, for Toby's sake.'

'Oh, I was most curious to meet you,' Helen assured her. 'When Dominic asked me to help, it was obvious he cares about you. I take it the feeling is mutual?'

'I respect Dominic very much,' Honor nodded.

'Who doesn't? The word I used was *care*.'

'Well, of course I care,' Honor nodded, feeling that she was damned if she was going to open the secrets of her heart to this woman. 'He's being very kind to me.

Helen lifted her chin to blow out a plume of blue smoke,

then quirked an eyebrow at Honor. 'You don't seem to mind my interrogating you.'

'Not at all,' Honor shrugged.

'You don't give me any answers, either,' Helen said with a quick smile. 'Even though you know exactly what I'm asking you.'

'Perhaps that's because I don't know the answers myself,' Honor said with an answering smile. 'And perhaps because I've been wondering the same things about you.'

'Then why don't we stop pussyfooting around?' Helen suggested, stubbing her cigarette out half-finished. 'I'm not Dominic's lover. Are you?'

'No,' Honor said, her cheeks colouring at the directness of the question.

'Odd,' Helen said, crossing her legs with a rustle of silk. 'I could have sworn you were. Although,' she said thoughtfully, dark eyes narrowed, 'now that I come to think of it, it's Dominic who gives that impression, not you. He looks at you like a lover. You look at him with rather more reserve than that.'

Honor interlaced her fingers, feeling that Helen Matthews was too damnably intelligent to spar with. Nor did she want to offend the woman who might well be Toby's only hope of staying out of jail. 'Dominic and I have had disagreements,' she said carefully. 'Not about Toby—about someone else close to me. He thinks he's right, and I think he's wrong, and—well, I'm afraid it's hopelessly complicated.' She made a little gesture. 'It isn't a straightforward relationship. In fact, I've never had a relationship quite like it before.'

Helen laughed softly. 'So that's how it is,' she murmured, studying Honor from under lowered lids. 'Well, well. I wonder if you know how many women would give their eye-teeth to be in your position? I don't think anyone has ever had Dominic Raven on a string in his entire life. It must be a new and not altogether pleasant experience for him.'

'I don't have Dominic on a string,' Honor said with a touch of irritation. 'He's not the sort of man any woman could keep on a string. Not for long, anyhow.'

'Not for long. My sentiments exactly,' Helen said with that same hint of inner amusement. 'I shall be most interested to see how things turn out.' She lit another cigarette, and Honor guessed that she used her chain-smoking as an outlet for nerves which never showed in her confident manner. 'How did you deal with the competition, may I ask?'

A loaded question! 'I'm sorry,' Honor replied gently, 'but I don't feel possessive enough about Dominic to regard other women as "competition".' Not yet, she added silently, at any rate.

'You surprise me,' she drawled back. 'Take my word for it, you have plenty of competition, whether you recognise it or not. I once took a notion for Dominic, as my mother would have put it, myself.'

'Once?' Honor couldn't resist echoing.

'Well, there's always hope,' Helen said sweetly. 'Though he never seems to notice my wiles. Or perhaps he's simply too well bred to notice what he doesn't want. Which I suppose,' she said through another cloud of smoke, 'officially makes me your rival.'

'Oh, no!' Honor said in distress.

'It won't affect your Toby,' Helen said drily. She glanced across the big room to where Dominic was coming back in. 'Come to think of it, it probably won't affect anything very much,' she said in an ever drier voice. 'I smoke too much, and I'm thirty-two, and I've already had one marriage go wrong. Dominic deserves a lovely, virginal, clear-skinned type. Like you.'

'Did I hear the word "virginal"?' Dominic enquired, sitting down between them.

'That's the one word you *would* pick up,' Helen snorted. Her eyes were warm though, but Dominic didn't seem to notice. Suddenly Honor felt a pang of compassion for rich, clever, beautiful Helen Matthews and her loving eyes. *My life is overcrowded with women like that,* he'd once told her. *They mean nothing to me.*

Compassion, yet there was also a flicker of joy which she couldn't suppress—joy that Dominic hadn't, after all, slept with this woman! 'I was saying that Honor has a virginal look.'

'Honor's a peach,' Dominic said with a smile that made her knees turn to water. He couldn't know, she thought with a touch of sadness, how Helen felt about him—or he would never had asked Helen to help. He must be blind to those wry smiles and almond eyes. What was this feeling inside? Was it exultation that Dominic had chosen her over someone as lovely and sophisticated as Helen? No, she wasn't mean enough to exult in that kind of triumph. Yet with her growing feelings for Dominic had come possessiveness.

And that, more than anything, ought to tell her what she really felt for him!

'Yes, she is rather.' Helen stubbed out her cigarette. 'Well, I think I can get a stay of execution on Toby until we can arrange a meeting to discuss him with the prosecutor involved. Shall I get in touch with you tomorrow, Dominic? You may have to meet me at fairly short notice.'

'No problem,' Dominic nodded. 'I think the cause is worth it.' He kissed Helen's cheek warmly. 'I appreciate your help,' he told her gently.

'*De nada,*' Helen said lightly. 'Must you go?'

'I'm afraid so,' Dominic said. 'It's been a long day.'

Outside, Helen took Honor's hand. 'I'll do my best,' she promised. 'Try not to worry in the meantime. Should Honor be on hand to make a special plea?'

'I don't think so,' Dominic shook his head.

'But I thought——' Honor began.

'It's better that you stay away,' he said firmly. 'There really isn't anything you can do to help.'

'Maybe he's right,' Helen said gently. 'It'll all work out. Goodnight, Honor.'

Honor kissed Helen's cool cheek, and they got into the car.

'Do you know she's in love with you?' Honor asked quietly, looking up at Dominic's face as they drove away.

'Helen?' He smiled as they walked to the Porsche. 'Don't be silly. I've known her for years. You look exhausted. Why not get some shut-eye while I drive you home?'

CHAPTER SIX

Mike Wetherall was at a conference on Friday, which was just as well, as she was hardly in the mood for explaining the previous day's emergencies to anyone—except Mark, to whom she gave a brief account. He was sympathetic, and approving of her choice of Dominic as an ally. Like her, his attitude towards Toby was one of compassion, rather than censure.

'Have you got the money to pay for this high-powered lawyer of Dominic's? Mark asked.

That had been exercising her thoughts, too. 'I should have enough tucked away. I hope. I really don't want Dominic to pay, and I've got a horrible feeling he's going to want to.'

'If you need any more,' he said gently, 'come to me first. And I mean that.'

'Thank you, Mark,' she said, almost on the verge of tears despite her smile. 'I appreciate it.'

'You're very worried,,' he sighed, leaning back behind his desk, 'aren't you?'

She nodded. Cocaine was going a bit far, even for Toby. But actually selling the stuff—she knew enough about the drugs scene to know that Toby already had one foot on a very slippery downward path. Please God, let Dominic get Toby out of this mess!

After work, she went across to Toby's flat, picked up some clothes and toiletries, and took them across to Finsbury Park.

Toby was looking slightly better, but he was very far

from his usual cocky self. She ascertained that he'd seen Dominic's lawyer, and hadn't yet been charged.

'Pru came in today,' Toby volunteered. 'She gave me hell.'

'Which is what you deserve.'

'She doesn't seem exactly pleased about Dominic helping me,' he mused. 'What's she got against him?'

'They've had a disagreement.' There had, in fact, been quite a storm yesterday when she'd confessed to Pru that she'd asked Dominic to help. Oddly enough, Pru's mood had improved dramatically over the past few days, giving Honor the hope that her sister might really be getting over Mog. But she could still hear Pru's anguished warning, *You'll end up regretting it, you mark my words!'*

'I'm relying on Dominic to get me out of this,' he said tightly. 'Don't let him forget me, sis!'

'I won't.' But what, she wondered, would happen to him, even if they did rescue him? His future seemed so gloomy and insecure, especially in the light of the cocaine episode. It was an awful sign of the dangers Toby was facing. If only he was more responsible, less self-pitying . . .

Toby was watching her face. 'Is Dominic sweet on you?' he asked suddenly.

'No,' she said quickly, taken by surprise.

'Then, what's in it for him?'

'I don't know,' she said uncomfortably. 'Nothing, I suppose.'

'Nothing?' he half smiled. 'Not even the heart of the criminal's grateful sister?'

'There might be a touch of that,' she admitted awkwardly. 'But don't say anything to Pru.'

'Ah.' He studied her lowered eyes and flushed cheeks for a moment. Only a year separated her and Toby, and he'd always understood her far better than Pru did. 'Pru also told me her marriage is off.'

'Yes.'

'Well, at least I know why she's been crying her eyes out for the past month,' he sighed. 'What caused the rift?'

'Oh—a quarrel.'

'But it's permanent?'

'Looks like it,' she nodded.

'Her family not good enough for him, is that it?'

The question was so close to the mark that Honor felt her cheeks flame. 'Don't be silly, Toby,' she said lightly. 'It was just incompatibility. She's been looking for another job over the past few days, which is a good sign. She's getting over it,' Honor smiled. 'I'm looking after her.'

'Yes. You're always looking after one or another of us, aren't you?' Toby took her hand across the table. 'Where would we be without you?'

When she got back to the flat, half an hour later, the news from Pru was slightly better.

'I've got a job.' Pru didn't sound very happy about it, but Honor perked up, glad to drag her thoughts away from Toby.

'Full-time?'

'Yeah.'

'Just like that? I'm so glad, Pru. Where at?'

'St Andrew's Stationery Supplies, off the Old Kent Road,' Pru said. 'Just basic secretarial stuff.' She sighed. 'The office is tiny, and the whole place smells of glue and brown paper.'

'Well, it's something.' She was secretly delighted at the news. Being among new people and having something to do with her time would work wonders for Pru. Honor pulled of her sweater, and walked through to her bedroom. 'When do you start?' she called.

'Next Monday.'

'Great.' Honor hunted for her hairbrush. It was missing off her dressing-table. Pru must have borrowed it as usual, so she went across the passage to Pru's bedroom. The hairbrush was lying on the bed.

Next to it were four opened envelopes. The American postmarks caught Honor's eye, and she picked one up idly. It was addressed to Pru, and the postmark clearly read 'New York'.

'Pru?' she called. 'Who are these letters from?'

Pru hurried into the bedroom, her expression one of dismay. 'They're just letters,' she said, scooping them up guiltily. 'Old letters from a friend.'

'But this is Mog's handwriting!' Honor let her sister snatch the envelope out of her hand, and stared at Pru in puzzlement. 'Has Mog been writing to you from New York? Why didn't you tell me?'

Pru didn't answer for a moment, tucking the letters away in her bedside drawer. When she turned back to Honor, her pretty face was pink. 'Promise you won't say anything to Dominic,' she pleaded.

'Is that why you didn't tell me?' Honor felt painful realisation dawn on her. 'Because you thought I'd tell Dominic the two of you were writing to each other?'

'Well, you and he are so close these days.' A touch sullenly, Pru lifted her chin. 'It's hard to tell where your loyalties lie any more.'

'Oh, Pru!' Honor sat on the bed, feeling like crying. 'Don't you trust me any more?'

'It's him I don't trust,' Pru said obstinately. 'He'd tell Mog's father. He's already broken me and Mog up once—he'd do it again if he knew!'

'I can hardly believe it,' Honor gasped. 'What's happened between us? After everything we've been to each other, you really thought I'd give your secrets away?'

Pru's set expression melted at the sight of Honor's distress. She sat down quickly beside her sister, and hugged her tight. 'Sis, don't look like that! I'm sorry, so sorry, I should have trusted you!' She kissed Honor's cheek resoundingly, then pulled the letters out of the drawer and offered them to Honor. 'Go on, read them!'

'I don't want to read them.' Honor sighed. 'I just feel so awful. I didn't know I'd lost your trust like that.'

'You haven't,' Pru said urgently. 'It's the other way round! I thought I'd lost *your* trust!'

'But why?' Honor asked incredulously. 'Why shouldn't I trust you?'

'Read Mog's letters,' Pru pleaded.

'They're private,' Honor said, shaking her head, and giving them back. 'Honestly, I don't want to read them. I'm just glad he's got in touch with you at last. What does he say?'

Pru looked down, her cheeks colouring slightly. 'That he loves me,' she replied in a low voice. She looked up, cheeks still pink. 'And I love him, Honor. I really do, with all my heart!'

'I believe you, piglet,' Honor smiled. 'At one time I thought you might be getting over Mog . . .'

'When I perked up?' Pru nodded vigorously. 'That was when I got his first letter. It was like a ray of sunshine! I thought he'd forgotten me.'

'It doesn't look like it,' Honor said gently.

'He wants to see me,' Pru said, pressing the sheaf to her cheek. 'He wants me to come to New York and stay with him.'

'What are you going to do?' Honor asked quietly.

'I'd give anything to go!' Pru got up restlessly, and put her letters away. 'I feel like I'm only half alive without him.

But what's the use of going if it's only going to mean more trouble for him? With both his father and Dominic against me, what chance have I got?'

'Dominic's not against you,' Honor said in surprise. 'Not actively, at any rate.'

Pru looked at her with worried eyes. 'What does he say about me?'

'We don't talk about you much,' Honor shrugged. 'It's a tender subject. But he just thinks you're too young and——' She remembered Dominic's suggestion that Pru didn't love Mog enough, but wisely held that back. '—well, not mature enough for marriage. That's all.'

'I *am* mature!' Once again, Pru was flushing hotly. 'Maybe I wasn't a few weeks ago, but I am now. I've never wanted anybody the way I want Mog!'

The telephone cut into Honor's reply. She got up absently and went into the hall to answer it.

The deep voice was Dominic's. 'Honor? You sound like a zombie.'

'Sorry.' She pushed her hair away from her face. 'I was miles away when I picked up the phone.'

'Toby's out of custody.'

'Dominic!' Her voice had risen to a yelp of delight, but he cut through fast.

'That doesn't mean he's free, Honor. Helen and I saw the police today, and it's unlikely now that they'll press for a conviction.'

'That's marvellous!'

'But he's still got to go to court.'

'Court?' she echoed, her delight slightly dampened.

'Yes. He's scheduled for a preliminary hearing some time next week. But there probably won't be a case. A report's gone in to the prosecutor's office this afternoon, and there's a good chance that the magistrate will release him with a caution.'

'Oh, Dominic.' Tension ebbed out of her, and she leaned against the wall tiredly.

'It's very promising,' he said, and she could hear the smile in the dark voice. 'I've just taken him over to his flat.'

'I'd better get round there,' Honor said protectively.

'No, you'd better not,' he said, and the command in his voice was steely. 'You're going to stay out of Toby's way for the next few days. He's got a lot of thinking to do, and he doesn't need your pity getting in his way. Now—can we talk about it over dinner tonight?'

'I'd love to,' she said eagerly.

'Can you be ready in half an hour?'

'Just about,' she said, glancing ruefully down at her creased office clothes.

'Good.' His voice took on a husky, warm note that melted her. 'I can't wait to see you.'

The line clicked dead in her ear. Honor turned to see Pru's pale face peering out of her bedroom door.

'I think Toby's going to be all right,' she said, and told Pru what Dominic had said.

'That's great,' Pru said, and straight afterwards, 'Is Dominic coming here?'

'Yes, he's taking me out to dinner in half an hour——'

'I don't want him to see me,' Pru said anxiously, and ducked back into her bedroom. When she reappeared, she was pulling on her coat.

'Pru! Stay and talk to Dominic——'

'Not ruddy likely! I'll go and see Caroline.' She gave Honor a quick hug, then hurried out of the door.

'Pru, you're being silly——'

'Enjoy yourself,' Pru called from the door. 'You deserve it.'

And Honor was alone.

From past experience she knew that Dominic would be punctual. There was no time for a major production, so she settled for a lightning shower, trying to rinse away the day's cares with the deliciously hot water. Prudence's words were going round in her head. Poor Pru! She was suffering a lot more than Honor had given her credit for. If only Dominic could see her, and judge her sincerity for himself. . . Honor wondered intently about the propriety of trying to persuade Dominic of Pru's real feelings for Mog Lambert.

She was still wearing nothing but lacy pink underwear when she heard the rumble of the Porsche in the mews outside. Muttering curses, she hauled on the evening dress she'd chosen as quickly as she could. The red silk gown was definitely the best thing she had, its thin straps showing off her pretty shoulders and its rich colour adding drama to her beauty; but she wasn't going to have much time for make-up.

She had to answer the doorbell in her bare feet, with her hair in a dark cloud around her face. She was hunched over one one side, struggling with a recalcitrant ear-ring, but even sideways-on, Dominic was stunningly handsome. His immaculate dinner-jacket contrasted strongly with the disarray that caused him to arch one eyebrow gently at her.

'I had no idea it was fancy dress,' he drawled. 'Presumably you're going as Orphan Annie?'

'I haven't had *time* to put my shoes on,' she wailed, leading him inside. 'I've just got in. And this blasted ear-ring——'

'Here.' Strong hands took over. She stood passively as he threaded the thin gold hoop through her ear. The closeness of him affected her strongly, as always; she could smell the faint musk of his aftershave, feel the warmth of his big body.

His black eyes were sultrily appreciative as they surveyed her. 'You look rather delicious, as it happens,' he purred softly. 'Where's Prudence?'

'Out,' Honor said briefly. Time enough to come to Prudence later in the evening.

'Is she?' he mused. 'Maybe we should open a tin of soup, and stay home instead?'

'I don't think so,' she said nervously. His smile was more in his eyes than on his mouth. He leaned forward to kiss the delicate lobe he'd just been adorning, then brushed his lips down the side of her neck.

'Dominic,' she began, 'I wanted to thank you for what you've done for my brother ...'

Her words trailed away. There was so much she wanted to say, but suddenly her mouth was dry, her pulses swollen with the rush of blood. It was happening all over again. Barefoot and tousle-haired, she felt herself melting into his arms as he kissed her throat, the fine curve of her jawline, the yielding softness of her mouth. God, he excited her; there was something in him, a quality she'd never felt before, that called to her innermost being.

His tongue probed her mouth hungrily, his hands sliding down her smooth flanks to meet on the small of her back, and pull her wickedly close to his hard strength. She was drowning in this erotic assault, all her defences melting before they'd even had a chance to harden ...

With a husky laugh, she laid shaky fingers over his mouth to forestall another kiss. 'Don't,' she said, and it was a plea. 'You make my head swim.'

'Is that so?' he grinned, beautiful white teeth glinting. 'I seem to have the same complaint. Maybe neither of us is well enough to go out.'

'I've had a long, hungry day,' she begged. 'I'm not going to be put off with Campbell's soup tonight, Dominic.'

His arms relaxed their hold. 'Pity,' he murmured, dark eyes unashamedly trailing down her body. 'My father always said women should be kept barefoot and pregnant. Seeing that you're already the one, it might be fun to try and make you the other.'

'*Dominic!*' She fled to her bedroom, giggling, and hunted for shoes on her hands and knees. 'I won't be a minute,' she called. 'There's sherry on the sideboard if you want a drink.'

'I'll wait,' he decided. It took her three minutes to pull on stockings and shoes, give her mouth and eyes the bare minimum of evening make-up, and brush her hair into a state of glossy order.

When she walked through into the living-room, Dominic was standing in front of her bookshelf, looking thoughtfully at the titles on the shelves. He turned, his eyes widening appreciatively as they took her in. 'What have you got in there?' he asked softly. 'Three maids and a couple of dressers? You look ravishing, green eyes.'

'I don't feel very ravishing,' she said shyly. He was the one who would dominate any crowd, she thought to herself. He was magnificently male, broad-shouldered and narrow-waisted, his height alone giving him instant star quality. 'What have you deduced from my books?'

'That there's a lot more to you than meets the eye.' He ran a finger along the spines. 'Shakespeare, Milton, Dickens. All the classics. You have a serious mind, Miss O'Hara. Then there are half a dozen works on computers and computing. That argues a dedicated approach to your work.'

'I like to keep informed,' she smiled.

'And then there's this section. Six books on alcoholism.' He glanced at her. 'Research on your father?'

'I thought I might be able to help, once,' she said sadly.

'That sounds like you,' he smiled. She shrugged awkwardly. He turned back to the books. 'Restoring antiques. Persian carpets. Do-it-yourself plumbing. Interior decorating. Even landscape gardening. Your interests are varied, indeed. Or are the glossy books just for show?'

'I love reading,' she answered him. 'And I can't afford to buy books for show. I could probably sit an exam on any of them. What you've done for Toby is wonderful,' she said, changing the subject. 'I don't know how to thank you.'

'He's not clear of the law yet,' Dominic reminded her. 'Besides which, that isn't the real problem. The real problem is what we're going to do with Toby after Thursday.'

'Yes. I've been thinking about that, too . . .'

'Funny,' he mused. 'Toby seems like your younger brother, somehow. I keep having to remind myself that he's a year older than you.'

'So does he, I think. He keeps forgetting that I'm his junior sister, and not his mother.' She gazed into the night beyond the window. 'Sometimes I despair of him, Dominic. I look at him, and I see Dad. I get so afraid that he'll turn out the same way . . .'

As he walked her to the car, he asked 'You're mother to both Pru and Toby, aren't you?' and glanced at her with a strange expression on his face—or was it just the softening effect of the darkness? 'You must have been looking after them both ever since you were ten years old.'

'It feels that way sometimes,' she laughed. She pulled her hair back, away from the delicate oval of her face. 'I've just been so much luckier than either of them. I was fourteen when my mother died. Toby was fifteen, Prudence eight. Middle children are often much less vulnerable than the youngest and oldest ones.'

He laughed softly, and she looked at him with quick eyes. 'Did I say something funny?'

'No. I just wonder where you get that sort of thing—middle children being less vulnerable.'

'It's true.'

'I know,' he nodded. 'But you're so young to be so wise, little one. And I'm not being patronising *or* sarcastic. Sometimes I think you're blessed with a real insight into human nature.' He glanced at her tenderly. 'You certainly know more about human nature than I did at twenty-five.'

Pleased with the compliment, Honor hesitated. 'I was talking to Prudence when you rang. Dominic, I think you're very wrong about her.'

'Oh?' His expression didn't change. 'In what way?'

'She really loves Mog,' Honor replied earnestly. 'She's ready for marriage, Dominic.'

'Love is not the only prerequisite for marriage,' Dominic smiled, as he steered the car out of the mews. 'Being in love and being married are quite different things.'

'But Pru——'

'Marriage calls for a commitment which Pru lacks almost completely,' Dominic cut through decisively. 'She's just a child, Honor.'

'Prudence stopped being a child a long time ago.' Honor said snappishly. 'I didn't think you were so unobservant!'

'Very well,' he said mockingly, 'your sister is fond of Mog Lambert, and she's sexually mature. Is that sufficient basis for a marriage?'

'Of course not,' she said patiently. 'But there are lots of other factors—such as Mog's own feelings. After all, he did propose to her. Why should *anyone*—even his own father—stand in his way?'

'That's a question you'll have to ask Morgan Lambert Senior,' Dominic pointed out with infuriating calm. 'You seem to think I'm personally responsible. I'm not. As it happens, I had very little to do with the whole business.'

'You're not very convincing,' Honor interrupted bitterly. 'It was your advice that really clinched it. If you hadn't advised Mog's father not to let the wedding go ahead, they'd probably be married by now.'

'May I remind you,' he said coolly, 'that your understanding of this affair is based on a handful of documents which you almost certainly don't understand—and which you should never have seen in the first place!'

'What difference does that make?' she demanded. 'All right, Pru was out of line when she took that file, but the situation really doesn't change. Separating two lovers out of snobbery still comes down to an ugly injustice.'

'I'll say it once more,' Dominic said, with a silky edge to his voice. 'When I wrote that I thought the marriage unsuitable, it was based on a personal assessment of your sister's character—and *not* on anything to do with her family connections. The fact that Morgan Lambert sent his son to America doesn't have anything to do with me. He didn't consult me, Honor—it was a family decision.'

Honor sat in silence for a while, aware of the futility of this argument. When she spoke again, her voice was quieter. 'What's happened has been a very big shock for Pru, Dominic. It may even have done some good, because she seems so much more adult these days. I wish you could see her, see how she's changed.'

He glanced at her ironically. 'Why are you telling me all this? You surely don't expect me to go to Morgan Lambert and try to change his mind?'

'Changing *your* mind would be enough for me,' she answered gently. 'I just don't want you to think the worst of Pru. At the moment, two young people who love each other very much are being kept apart——'

He laughed in mock surrender. 'All right. If you really think Pru's changed, then I'll accept your judgement. But no more now. We'll discuss it later,' he promised, 'and you can ladle on the whitewash. OK?'

'OK!'

They were heading north, leaving the traffic behind them. 'I hope you're hungry?' he asked.

'Starving,' she nodded.

'Good.' He accelerated hard down the street, the power of the car pushing her back into the leather seat like a giant hand. 'I want you to enjoy tonight.'

CHAPTER SEVEN

HONOR laid her knife and fork down reluctantly, and sighed. 'I really couldn't eat another thing. I think that's the best meal I've ever had.'

'I'm glad.' Dominic smiled at her, the candle flames reflected in his dark eyes. 'You look tired. Maybe you ought to have been in bed hours ago.'

'Oh no,' she said anxiously, sitting forward. 'I'm enjoying myself far too much!' She'd never been taken to a place like this in her life before. The restaurant overlooked the Thames, and its atmosphere of old-world elegance had charmed her right from the start. The garden outside the big glass doors had been lit by experts, giving an enchanted view down to the darkly glinting river.

It had been a superb meal, starting with grouse cooked on the spit with garlic and bacon; followed by the first roast pheasant of the year, together with autumn vegetables; and concluded by a dizzyingly exotic pudding of fruit in liqueur with whipped cream. That last, aided and abetted by the unmistakably vintage Châteauneuf, had brought a wave of slightly unreal sleepiness over her just now, but the last thing she wanted was to give Dominic the impression she was about to nod off. 'Do you often eat here?'

'On special occasions.'

'Is this a special occasion?' she asked.

'It is for me,' Dominic said gently. He poured more wine into her glass, waving away the waiter who'd materialised to do the job for him.

They were so close tonight, with a special intimacy that thrilled her. She was coming to know this tall, dark man, coming to understand the way he thought and acted. There was sternness, even harshness in him, yet there was also great kindness and gentleness.

And with her understanding, her love for him was deepening. The more she knew about him, the more she wanted to know; it was a kind of hunger to find out all she could about him.

He'd explained to her how he and Helen Matthews had put a convincing case forward for Toby being treated as someone in need of help, rather than punishment. In the meantime, Toby would be meeting a specialist for assessment, and with luck, there would be enough evidence to convince the magistrate that Toby should not face charges.

They'd also talked about Pru, and though he'd listened to her defence of her sister, she knew that, inside, his original judgement was far from shaken. It wasn't easy to accept that someone she respected as much as Dominic could have such a low opinion of Pru; nor could she share Dominic's calm assurance that a little worry and suffering would do Toby's soul good. She was far too protective about both of them to be that dispassionate . . .

'You know just about everything about my family,' Honor smiled. 'Let's talk about yours for a change.'

'What do you want to know?' he invited.

'Are your parents alive?' she ventured.

'They're both alive, yes, and living happily in Northumberland. Like you, I have a brother.' A smile edged his mouth. 'I also have five sisters.'

'Five!' She had to laugh. 'Somehow, I never saw you as coming from a big family.'

'The Ravens are quite a clan,' he assured her. 'Most of my sisters are older than I am, and four of them are married with children, so Christmas is quite a show.'

'I'll bet it is.' She grinned. 'Fancy growing up with five

sisters! Now I know why you've got such a confident air with women. I suppose they spoiled their handsome younger brother rotten?'

'They still do,' he nodded. 'Not that we exactly lived in luxury in those days. My father was the village policeman, and his salary didn't go far among seven children.'

'It doesn't seem to have done you any harm,' she commented, glancing at the breadth of his shoulders. 'And do you all get on with each other?'

'Like a house on fire,' Dominic smiled. 'We're close without being on top of each other all the time. One of my sisters lives in America, another one works in France. But we see each other as often as we can—and we all meet up at Christmas, no matter what.'

'That sounds marvellous.' Honor said wistfully. She cupped her chin in her hands, looking at him with slightly melancholy green eyes. 'If only you knew how lucky you were, Dominic. I'd have given anything to have had a family like that, close and loving ...'

He reached out to draw a finger smilingly down her nose. 'Don't look so dismal,' he said tenderly. 'The obvious answer is to have a family of your own, not so? Then you can make sure there aren't any mistakes.'

'I suppose so.' But his words had reminded her painfully of the dreams she'd had to part with when Mog had left for America. Not wanting sadness to break into the blissful intimacy of this moment, she changed the subject. 'Was that why you went into security—because your father was a policeman?'

'Indirectly,' he nodded. 'I came down to the Big Smoke at eighteen, determined to do something spectacular with my life.' He turned his wine glass in strong elegant fingers. 'I suppose I just wanted to make a lot of money at first. I had a flair for electronics, and I'd designed a new kind of burglar alarm. In my innocence,' he smiled, 'I imagined that I'd already made my fortune. I expected all the burglar-alarm companies to be falling over themselves to buy the patent.'

'But they weren't?' she asked.

'They weren't remotely interested.'

'What did you do?'

'I bought a derelict workshop,' he said calmly, 'and started manufacturing them myself, with a staff of unemployed electricians. Then I launched a small firm to market and install the things. People liked them, so it wasn't very long before Raven Security was in business in a big way.'

'Just like that?' she said in awe.

'More or less.' He signalled to the waiter for coffee. Honor watched his tanned, incredibly handsome face. Things came so easily to him, she thought wryly. He had strength and capability that went a long way beyond the ordinary man.

'The security business has changed radically since then,' he said, over the rich Turkish coffee. 'And not altogether for the better. When I started out, people simply wanted to defend their property and personnel from villains.' His deeply carved mouth curved into an expression of distaste. 'These days everyone's rushing down technical blind alleys, chasing real or imaginary enemies. Electronic surveillance, spectrum chromotography, computer crime. You'd be astounded at the things people ask security firms to do. And the private individual has taken security up in a big way, too, as you've already found out.' He smiled drily at her as she winced.

'The darker side of security?' she suggested.

'That's a good way of putting it. They want to check out their husbands, fiancées, employees, even their children. It's becoming quite common for an engaged couple to check each other out, check each other's families out, then sign a ten-page premarital contract specifying what happens to their money in the event of a divorce. In the event of their actually getting married after all that,' he went on ironically, 'and staying married long enough to have any children, they'll most likely turn to a security company to put their children under surveillance. Check out their private lives, political affiliations, whether they're using drugs or not. It's a cosy feeling, being secure.'

'And doesn't all that sicken you?' she asked quietly.

'Sure it sickens me,' he said with a dry note in his voice. 'That's why I don't usually touch it! That wasn't what I envisaged when I started out, fifteen years ago now.'

'Fifteen years ago. Which makes you——' She calculated silently. 'Thirty-three.'

'Give or take a year,' he nodded. 'Eight years older than you. Does that intimidate you?'

'I suppose it does,' she confessed wryly.

'You think I'm too old?' he suggested, one eyebrow lifting casually.

'I think *I'm* too young,' she corrected him. 'When I'm with you, I feel like——' She hesitated, then found the phrase she'd thought of earlier on. '—like a babe in the woods.'

'With me cast as the wicked wolf?' he enquired drily. 'I had no idea you found me so threatening.'

'Now I've offended you,' she said unhappily. 'I don't find you threatening. If anything, I find you all too——' The wine had loosened her tongue, and she tried to gulp back the words. 'I—I don't find you frightening, that's what I mean.'

'All too attractive?' he said in a velvety voice. 'Is that what you were going to say?'

'I think I've had too much wine,' she laughed breathlessly. 'I wouldn't take anything I say too seriously tonight if I were you.'

'You puzzle me,' he said softly. 'You acknowledge the

fact that you're attracted to me, but you treat it as though it were something better not mentioned. As though I were some sort of dangerous drug.' His mouth curved in a bitter smile. 'Is that because you find me unacceptable as a potential lover?'

'That isn't a fair question,' she said in a low voice, looking down.

'You frustrate me,' he said with a hint of harshness in his deep voice. 'That makes me unfair.' He watched her downcast eyes for a moment, then relaxed, and reached for her hand across the table. 'I'm sorry. You're very tired, and I'm keeping you out of your bed far too long. Shall we go?'

'If you like,' Honor nodded, glad to be off the hook.

Dominic paid the bill with a credit card, and a few minutes later they were driving out of the car park in the direction they'd come. She glanced at her watch. It wasn't yet ten.

They drove through the dark streets, listening to the smooth jazz from the Porsche's hi-fi.

'Are you still hunting for the mole at ComTech?' she asked dreamily. 'Or can we sleep peacefully in our beds now?'

'You think it's all rather silly, don't you?' he remarked, giving her a quick glance from under lowered brows. 'Taking precautions, maintaining controls. Security procedures annoy you, don't they?'

'Well, I can think of some people they annoy more than me,' she shrugged. 'But they're not universally popular, no.'

'And what if I told you that the jobs of everyone at ComTech—including yours—depended on those controls?'

'That's very dramatic,' she smiled. But something in the way he'd said it had made her uneasy, and she looked at him uncertainly. 'Isn't it?'

'You know the current profit and loss situation better

than anyone,' Dominic said obliquely. 'How well is the company doing?'

'Not as profitably as when I first joined it,' she admitted, 'but it doesn't do too badly.'

'With a million and a half pounds' worth of unsold word processors lying in a warehouse in Kent?' he enquired.

'Oh, the LP-550 will pick up,' she said confidently.

'No, it won't,' he contradicted her calmly. 'According to the Blair-Winship report, the LP-550 is never going to sell more than a third of its originally projected figures. That's because someone stole the design, Honor. Someone lifted the most important data about the LP-550 right out of one of the banks, and sold it to the opposition.'

The look she gave him was unhappy. 'How can you be so sure?'

'Because the LP-550 contained several unique features,' he said grimly. The black Porsche swooped down fast into a tunnel, making Honor's stomach jump uncomfortably inside her. 'Features that Mark and his boffins had developed themselves. Features that just couldn't have appeared by coincidence in not one, but *two* rival machines launched at the same time. And the data was stolen right at the planning and forecasting stage, a long time ago.'

'By whom?' she challenged uneasily.

'A ComTech employee.'

'I can't believe that,' she said decisively. 'None of the people I know at ComTech would ever do such a thing. Why should they want to see the company go down?'

'Personal profit. Maybe they think their salaries aren't good enough, maybe they dream of a life-style beyond their reach.' He shook his head. 'Information like that is worth big money, Honor. It's worth big risks. And ComTech, unfortunately, happened to be one of the most poorly guarded firms in the industry.'

'Mark's a scientist,' she sighed, 'not a businessman.'

'Exactly,' Dominic nodded. 'He's having to learn the hard way.'

'But if the damage has already been done, why do our jobs depend on security measures?'

He swung the car on to a slip-road, and into the tree-lined streets of an exclusive suburb. 'You really don't know?' he queried gently.

'Don't know what?'

'About Mark's new project.'

'I haven't heard a thing,' Honor replied in genuine surprise. 'What kind of project?'

'That's classified information,' he grinned. 'Can't tell you a thing.'

'You don't suspect *me*?' she yelped as the idea suddenly occurred to her.

'Of course I suspect you,' Dominic retorted calmly. He gave her appalled face an amused glance from the tails of his eyes, and lowered his voice to a passable impersonation of Maigret's. ' I suspect *everybody*.'

'Oh, Dominic,' she groaned. 'I thought you were serious for a moment!'

'The project really is top secret,' he smiled. 'Not just to guard it against prying eyes, either. Mark's putting in a bid for an RAF contract. A computerised war-games system, a kind of highly sophisticated training aid for jet-fighter pilots.'

'Wow!'

'Wow, indeed. If his system is successful, it could pull ComTech right out of the junior league, and into the national league.'

'I had no idea,' she said, still taking it in.

'That's right,' he said significantly. 'You have no idea. You didn't even hear what I haven't just told you.'

'I won't breathe a word,' she promised. She felt a glow inside, though, that he'd trusted her with information of that kind. 'Thank you for telling me,' she said quietly. 'It really is exciting news.'

'Let's hope Mark gets that contract. He's been working flat out for a long time now.'

'I thought he looked awfully preoccupied,' she remembered. 'But I assumed that was just because of the LP-550. So *that's* why security has been stepped up. Did he call you in specifically because of the new project?'

'When the report confirmed the likelihood of a leak within the company,' Dominic nodded. 'He realised that he simply couldn't take any more chances. And that's why all your jobs depend on improved security.' She digested that in a rather shamefaced silence, as he went on, 'To answer your original question—I've done what I could to tighten things up, so the initial phase is over. But as for "the mole", as you call him—yes, of course it would be important to pinpoint him. Or her. On the other hand, it's far more important to safeguard the future prosperity of the company.'

The lights were on in the flat when he pulled up in the mews later on. Dominic glanced up with a half-smile. 'I notice that Pru has been treating me like a leper lately, so I won't come up,' he said. 'But I've listened to what you said tonight, and I promise not to have any more prejudices.' He drew her close, kissing her soft mouth and caressing her hair with gentle hands. 'Can I see you at the weekend?'

'Yes,' she whispered, lost in the nearness of him.

'I'd like you to come to my home. You've never seen it. I'll pick you up tomorrow lunch time from work—all right?'

'I'd love that,' she nodded, staring up at him.

'Good. Now get your delicious self up to bed, and I'll see you tomorrow.'

Mike Wetherall was standing at the lifts in the lobby as she pushed through the revolving doors on Saturday morning. He held the lift door open for her.

'What happend on Thursday?' he asked, his normally deadpan face concerned.

'A domestic emergency.' She really didn't want to explain to Mike, so she tried hard to smile it off. 'A relation of mine got into a spot of bother.'

He stabbed the key for the fifth floor, and the lift hummed into action. 'Nothing serious, I hope?'

'He's all right now. I think.'

'Good.' Mike glanced at her, still looking concerned. 'Can I talk to you for a moment, Honor? In your room?'

'Of course,' she nodded, trying to make it sound sincere. She had a lot of work to catch up on, and in any case she didn't want company right now, but Mike's expression was pregnant with important things. 'Though do you mind if we pick up some coffee from the machine first? I'm dying for something hot.'

'I'll join you,' he sighed, 'though that stuff does nothing for me. Machine coffee is the original cup that cheers but not inebriates. I couldn't help hearing the office gossips,' Mike continued, as they walked into her office five minutes later. 'They say you spent the day with Dominic Raven on Thursday.'

'Oh.' Damn the office gossips! There didn't seem much else to be said, so Honor just drank her coffee and waited.

'We don't normally discuss our private lives in this place, do we? We're all very impersonal and efficient. But I've known you a long time, Honor. I hope that gives me the right to offer you a piece of maybe impertinent and unwelcome advice.'

'Go ahead,' she said, glancing at him. He was very serious, not even a poetic quotation in sight. He'd had his fair hair cut even shorter than usual, and it gave him a curiously old-fashioned look, a crew-cut kid from the 1950s who'd never grown up.

'Whatever your domestic emergency is—and I'm not

prying, believe me—it seems you've asked Dominic Raven to help you. But he's a pretty formidable proposition, you know. He doesn't exactly have a reputation as the loyal, loving type.'

'I didn't know he had any sort of reputation,' Honor said uneasily.

'You may be a very bright young lady,' Mike said gently, 'but you are rather naïve as far as men go.'

'Am I?' She sipped her coffee. 'Do you know something about Dominic Raven that I don't?'

'It seems that almost everyone knows more about Dominic Raven than you do,' Mike smiled. 'I'm not one for spreading gossip, you know that. I wouldn't say anything if I didn't have the impression you were getting involved with Mr Raven in an emotional way.'

'Go on,' Honor invited quietly.

'He's ruthless, Honor. There are men—and women too, for that matter—who've had bitter experience of that.' Mike drained his cup with an expression of distaste. 'People who get involved with Dominic Raven have a way of ending up on the scrap heap. Picked up, used, then discarded.'

'That's a nasty accusation!'

'Dominic Raven's one of the most successful men in the security field,' Mike said steadily. 'But fifteen years ago, he was a nobody. He latched on to an inventor called Jeremy Larkin, who'd just developed a revolutionary kind of burglar alarm. Raven talked Larkin into taking him on as a partner somehow; then Raven did the ultimate cuckoo-in-the-nest job on his kindly patron. The design was all Larkin's, but somehow Raven wound up with the patent. He wound up with all the money, too, and before long Jeremy Larkin lost his share to Dominic Raven. Raven couldn't get rid of him fast enough—more or less slammed the door in his face. The end result was that Jeremy committed suicide, owing thousands, two years later—and Dominic Raven didn't even go to the funeral.'

Honor felt the chill spreading through her, as though she'd swallowed ice. She thought of the way Dominic had described his start in business, without the slightest mention of a partner of any sort. The two versions were utterly different—yet she'd worked with Mike for four years now—and she knew he wouldn't be saying anything as horrible as this if there weren't at least a grain of truth in it. 'How do you know all this—that it's not just a bit of ugly gossip?'

'I happen to have been around then,' Mike said quietly. 'Forgive me, but you were still in pigtails at the time. There's no exaggeration in the story, believe me.'

'I see.' Honor stared blankly into space, trying to assimilate what she'd just heard. Disbelief was her initial reaction, yet Mike's expression was totally sincere.

'His reputation with women isn't much better,' Mike went on. He glanced at her pale face sympathetically. 'Raven goes through females the way some people go through cigarettes. He's a beautiful animal, I grant you, but he's said to be plain insatiable. It's almost a pathological thing with him.'

'I see,' she said again. Honor felt sick now, as though she'd opened a drawer to find an adder coiled up inside. How horrible, if it were true. And how horrible, if it were true, that she'd involved herself and Toby with a man like that.

'I realise that he could be very attractive to you,' Mike said. 'But he has a pretty fearsome reputation. I really would hate to see you get involved with him. Just a word of warning, Honor. You were made for love and romance. Not for men like Dominic Raven. We'll drop the subject, because I can see it's upset you.' He nodded at her ID badge. 'I see you've been tagged as well. Welcome to Sing Sing.'

'It feels a bit like that,' she agreed, still feeling faint with disillusionment. She made an effort to sound normal. 'According to Mrs Lindsay, it's more or less standard procedure these days.'

'She ought to know,' Mike smiled. 'She must see more dusty offices in a week than you or I could shake a stick at. But I still don't like it.'

'Nor do I,' Honor had to admit, putting down her half-full cup. Suddenly she couldn't drink any more. She swung on her chair to face the screen. 'Thank you for that warning, Mike. I—I appreciate the thought.'

'I wouldn't want to see those pretty green eyes any sadder than they are just now.' Mike took off his horn-rims and polished them thoughtfully on his tie. 'As a matter of fact, though, there are a lot of things I don't like about the way this firm is turning out.'

Honor was already switching on her computer, and praying Mike would just go now, and leave her to her work, and her bruised emotions.

'I take it you haven't heard the latest? No one's allowed to use terminals after closing time or at weekends any more. Anyone caught *in flagrante delicto* will be subject to dismissal. How's that for motivation?'

Honor shook her head. ComTech was a computer firm, and most of its staff were computer enthusiasts. It had always been tacitly accepted that anyone could use the terminals after hours, as long as it was for company business. 'I really can't chat any longer,' she said apologetically, sliding the diskettes into the disk-drive unit. 'I've got so much to get through.'

'Ditto.' Mike rose and walked to the door. He hovered on the lintel for a moment before closing her door, 'Thanks for giving me a hearing, Honor. I'm sorry if I've upset you.'

She just smiled tightly, her fingers busy on the keys. The columns of figures flickered across the screen. But with one part of her mind she was going over and over what Mike had told her about Dominic. It seemed too ugly to be true; and yet she herself had been all too aware of the man's driving virility. It wasn't impossible to imagine his dominant personality ousting a weaker, more yielding partner, leaving him broken behind on the path to success. Nor was it difficult to imagine him as a Don Juan, devouring women remorselessly and without emotion . . .

What did that mean to her? It was clear that Mike was warning her to have nothing to do with Dominic. But even if that were feasible, would she want to take that advice? It was a question that continued to haunt her thoughts right up until lunch time, when she locked her office, and went down to wait for Dominic in the car park.

The drive beyond the high wrought-iron gates led up through a surprisingly extensive garden to a long, low, ultra-modern house with a sweeping, tiled roof, set on a slight natural rise. As Dominic drove the Porsche into an underground garage, the doors of which had opened to a touch on a command module. Honor had time to see that the architecture of the house was strikingly individualistic.

The garage was huge, and contained two other cars, one of them a vintage red sports car. It was also spotless, from its laid-brick floor to its brilliantly lit ceiling. As she stepped out in awe, she could see that part of the area was given over to a workshop, filled with highly complex electronic gear.

'This is straight out of the twenty-first century!' she exclaimed.

Dominic smiled, tall and potently handsome, and took her arm. 'You're worth impressing,' he responded to her praise. 'Come and see the rest of the house.'

The wide staircase opened out at the top, revealing a living area that was at least twice the size of Honor's whole flat. It was exquisitely appointed, with the minimum of space given to unnecessary clutter, and the maximum freedom given to the natural materials of wood, marble and sandstone which had been used for the structure. She walked silently across the glowing golden-oak floor, taking in the vivid blues and creams of three big, modern paintings, the massive cactus that towered out of a pot, the shelves of books that covered one entire wall.

'I had no idea . . .' she breathed. 'It's so beautiful, Dominic. Who designed the house?'

'My brother, Larry.' He led her to the sunken conversation area, which contained a suite of white hide furniture. 'He's rather gifted, don't you think?'

'He's very brilliant,' she said decisively. Everything in the house was subtle, nothing obvious or garish, and yet the whole effect was stunning, on a grand scale. She glanced at Dominic's tall figure as he pulled off his jacket and loosened his tie. He moved with such pantherlike grace that he made other men look clumsy beside him. The house was a perfect setting for him, she thought instinctively. A big house for a big man. 'Your brother must be a very sucessful architect.'

'Public buildings are more his usual field—he did this house as a special favour. But yes, Larry's much in demand.' Dominic opened the door of a black-lacquered cocktail cabinet. 'A drink?'

'Something very light,' she said, all too aware of her need to stay alert. She sank gratefully into the white leather sofa, watching him mix the drinks. 'Are all your family high achievers—like you and Larry?'

The muscles in the tanned column of his throat rippled as he laughed softly. 'I don't know whether Larry or I would ever described ourselves as "high achievers". I suppose we were all taught the virtues of hard work at an early age. My father is a perfectionist, a man with an infinite capacity for detail. The perfect policeman, in fact. We all picked that up in our own way.' He passed her the tall, cool drink, and nodded at the sofa she was sitting on. 'My sister Sarah made this suite. She and Vanessa run a furniture design centre in Newcastle. None of the other three are in business—they're too busy with family life.'

'It's hard to believe you've built everything up all on your own,' she said casually. 'Did you never have a partner of any sort?'

'A partner?' he repeated with a quirk of one eyebrow. 'What makes you ask that?'

'Nothing in particular,' she lied convincingly. 'Just wondering.'

'I told you how the business started the other night,' he smiled. 'It was one per cent inspiration, and the rest damned hard work.'

She just smiled at him, but it was a smile that hid pain. Why hadn't he so much as mentioned the other man? Either he was lying deliberately, or he'd convinced himself that he really *had* done it all himself, conveniently forgetting all about Jeremy Larkin.

It depressed her badly. If he was ruthless in business, then he would be ruthless in love, too. And that meant that Mike Wetherall's warning had to be taken seriously indeed.

All around her she could see the evidence of that formidable energy which had struck her about him from the start. It was very hard to believe, as she studied his face and hands now, that Dominic Raven was a man who could be satisfied by one woman. Why should he? she thought sadly. He lived in a different world from most people. If he had the drive to cope with a massively profitable business and a passionate sex-life, then who was she to disapprove? She felt that touch of sadness again, making her mouth droop at the corners. Business could be a rough, cruel world, she knew that. Yet she'd felt that Dominic Raven was different from the rest . . .

'That isn't bad,' Honor said, shaking her head, 'for the children of the village bobby.'

'My father didn't stay as village bobby all his life.' Dominic said. He toasted her with a glint in his black eyes. 'He retired a Commissioner.'

'Oh,' Honor said, abashed. He was laughing again as he sat down beside her.

'You're so transparent sometimes,' he said softly, eyes warm on her. 'Your every emotion shows in your face. It makes you very tempting to tease.'

'I'm never quite sure when you are teasing me,' she confessed in a small voice, 'and when you're serious. You must have wonderful Christmases together, all of you.'

'Will you come up this Christmas?' he asked matter-of-factly. 'Come up to Northumberland and share it with us?'

'Now you *are* teasing me,' she smiled.

'No, he said gently, 'now I'm being serious.' Honor looked into Dominic's deep eyes, her smile fading at what she saw there. 'I don't think you know quite how serious I am about you,' he said in a husky voice that brought goose-flesh trickling across her skin.

'Dominic,' she said, her mouth suddenly dry. 'I—I don't know what to say. I'm very honoured. B-but . . .'

'Your sister and brother can spare you for once,' he purred. 'It's doubtful whether either of them would even notice you were gone.'

'That's not fair,' she defended them weakly. 'They need me. Give—give me some time to think about it, Dominic.'

'The cautious Miss O'Hara,' he said with an expression of disgust.

'There was a young lady of Niger,' Honor recited poker-faced, 'who rode with a smile on a tiger. I'm sure you know the rest of it.'

'I do,' he agreed. 'But I can hardly have my wicked way with you on the hearthrug in front of my assembled family, can I? After all, my mother is chairwoman of the local Woman's Institute.'

'Is she? My mother was in the WI too,' she smiled.

His eyes were smoky. 'You're so beautiful when you smile, Honor. Especially when you smile like that.' He reached out to brush her hair back, in that tender gesture she'd come to know so well. It was stupid to pretend she was cool about him any more. She needed him, needed him more and more with each day that passed. And today he was so beautiful in that intensely masculine way that always made her heart flip right over inside her. At the neck of his opened shirt, the crisp black hair curled around the muscular base of his throat, infinitely suggestive of his physical and sexual potency. His was a mouth to command, imperious and sensual. Its warmth so often undercut the icy brilliance of those black eyes, even when he was being most stern with her.

Whether she leaned forward at that moment, or whether he drew her, she couldn't tell; but before she could stop herself with any sensible alarm bells, she was melting into his arms, her mouth parting helplessly for his kiss.

CHAPTER EIGHT

It was so easy to leave all her reservations and fears behind her, and just lose herself in Dominic's passion. His kiss was more intoxicating than any wine they'd drunk tonight, his mouth firm and strong and gentle. Honor clung to him with trembling eagerness, her need for him flooding her. Every time this happened between them, her reactions grew more intense. Once she'd thought that he was too male to ever become really close to her, that she could only ever grow truly near to someone gentle and tender.

But that wasn't true. She was starting to realise that Dominic's very maleness drew her like a magnet, calling to some deep inner feelings of her heart. Dominic's strength, Dominic's potent will, the way he protected her, the way he dominated her—it all excited her beyond anything any man had ever achieved.

'You're so lovely,' he whispered.

As she arched to him, revelling in the strong hands that caressed her slender back, she knew that no matter what the danger, there was no way she could resist this feeling.

But misgivings didn't stay long in her thoughts. There was room for nothing but Dominic, for the way his mouth and hands were worshipping her body. She felt no shame as he peeled the clinging red gown away from the gentle swell of her breasts, baring them to his touch.

She ran trembling fingers through the thick curls of his hair as he bent his head to her, his lips brushing the jutting peaks of her nipples with almost unbearable tenderness.

'I want you, Honor.' His voice was a warm caress in the valley between her breasts. 'I've wanted you from the moment our eyes met in that boardroom.'

'I can't understand it,' she whispered. She caressed his cheek, studying his mouth with adoring eyes. 'I used to think I detested you. Now I don't know what I feel towards you.' Her lips clung to his, as though reluctant to end their kiss. 'You make me feel so . . . confused . . .'

'I'm not confused at all,' he smiled. His fingertips trailed across her thigh, sending a new wave of feeling spreading through her loins. 'I know exactly what I want to do to you, Honor. Right here and now.'

'But I'm not ready——' she said unsteadily.

'Yes you are,' he murmured, his mouth seeking hers. She moaned softly as his fingers stroked the smooth inner skin of her thigh, higher and higher, until his caress reached the taut satin of her panties. She'd never felt anything like this sweet agony before. She moaned softly as his hand cupped the mound of her sex possessively, a caress that was both protective and achingly sexual.

'Dominic, *no* . . .' An ecstasy of giddiness washed over her as his fingers moved beneath the flimsy material to touch her melting womanhood.

Her body moved languorously in his arms, her thighs trapping his hand as she twined her arms round his neck. '*Please!*' she whispered, green eyes half-veiled by her thick black lashes. 'Please stop now, Dominic . . .'

'You're tormenting me,' he said huskily. 'I need you with all my soul, darling.'

'Oh, Dominic . . .' Like a child, she pulled the straps of her gown up over her shoulders, covering her breasts again. 'Please respect what I ask!'

'You're making it very difficult for me.' he said grimly. 'If I didn't know you better, I'd say you were just playing with me!'

Tautly, he rose and walked across the room. Honor brushed her hair away from her face, feeling the acute pang of losing him spread through her body. He leaned on the window sill, staring out, the way he'd once done in her office.

'Maybe you think I do this casually,' he said quietly. 'I don't. I don't feel this way with other women, Honor. You do something to me that is very special.'

Words that made her heart jump inside her. Or were they just routine, the words he said to every woman he wanted? 'Oh, come,' she said with a bittersweet smile, 'you must make love to dozens of women.'

'I'm not a libertine,' he said roughly glancing at her over his shoulder.

'How can you not be, with so many women falling over themselves to get to you?'

'I come from a family of five sisters, Honor.' His eyes held hers steadily. 'I like women. I like them and respect them. Not all men do. But I wouldn't tell you that you were special to me if I didn't mean it.'

'I'm sorry if I offended you,' she said, risng to go to his side on legs that felt weak. 'I just wonder how long I would stay special to you once you'd possessed me.'

'There's only one way to find out,' he said with a faint smile.

'Yes.' She hugged his slim, strong waist, leaning her cheek against his shoulder. He smelled so good, warm and male and clean. 'But that's a rather drastic way. I'd prefer something a little more—experimental.'

'You want to put me on trial before you'll come to my bed?' he enquired, one eyebrow arching dangerously.

Honor shook her dark head hastily. 'That sounds horrible! I just want to give us a—a little more time.'

'A little more time,' he repeated, holding her gaze. 'And then, green eyes, I'll wait no longer.'

'That bloody man!' Joanna fumed. 'I wonder if he knows

just how difficult he's made life for everyone in this office.' She glared at Honor with big blue eyes. 'I've just been up to Records to get some files, and the old witch in charge wouldn't give them to me. She said I needed written clearance from Mark. *Clearance*, I ask you! Of course, Mark happens to be in Kent all this week, so it means I just have to wait——' She drew a deep breath. 'It makes me so angry to be *mistrusted*, after all the years I've worked for this company.'

'It's not personal,' Honor tried to soothe Joanna. 'Everybody gets rubbed the wrong way a little with all these procedures. New systems always chafe a bit, don't they?'

'I'll tell you what chafes a bit,' Joanna retorted, 'and that's Dominic Raven,' Joanna was one of those lucky people who got prettier as they got angrier; Honor had to bite back a smile as she admired Joanna's pink cheeks and sparkling eyes. 'I really hate him. He's a thoroughly wicked man.'

'That's going a bit far, isn't it?' Honor soothed.

'He's the most ruthless, arrogant man in London,' Joanna crackled. She gave Honor a sharp look. 'And you're a fool for getting involved with him.'

Honor's smile faded. 'I take it you've been listening to office gossips as well,' she said coolly.

'I've been using my own eyes,' Joanna retorted. 'He's singled you out, Honor. You're just a way for him to get his hooks into ComTech.' She sat up very straight. 'I'm sorry,' she concluded stiffly, 'but I happen to like you, and you ought to be told that you're being used.'

'Used?' She thought of the way Dominic was helping Toby, but couldn't very well say anything to Joanna about that. 'Actually, he's been very kind to me, Joanna. I think you're wrong about him.'

'Listen to me,' Joanna's face showed the depth of her feelings as she fixed Honor's eye. 'Dominic Raven has been using everyone around him all his life. His reputation is bad, bad, bad. He had a partner called Jeremy Larkin, whom he exploited and then destroyed——'

'I've also heard that horror story,' Honor cut through tensely, not wanting to hear it again.

'It's no horror story,' Joanna warned sharply. 'It's the truth. Jeremy was a brilliant man, Honor. *He* wouldn't believe that Dominic was using him, either. When he learned the truth, it was too late.'

'I don't think I'm that innocent,' Honor said calmly. 'I would know if I was being used.' But her heart was sinking at Joanna's vehemence.

'Listen,' the other woman said wearily, 'do you really think you're the first woman who's been romanced by Dominic Raven? London is littered with his conquests, kiddo. Oh yes, he's quite a stud, and he's got a magnificent body. But women don't mean anything to him. He used to be able to pick them up, bed them, and discard them.' She pulled an ugly face. 'Trouble is, his reputation's getting around these days. So he has to play it softly-softly. Champagne dinners and bunches of red roses, and a show of dripping sincerity. But the end result's still the same—he leaves them flat for the next pair of high heels that crosses his path.'

Honor walked across to the window, feeling sick inside. She was used to Joanna's terminology, in which people 'bedded' one another, and no detail was too private to mention; but it gave her a nauseous ache to hear that sort of thing said about Dominic.

'Sorry,' Joanna concluded vigorously, 'but Dominic Raven is definitely not to be trusted within ten miles of a decent woman.'

Honor rubbed her temples tiredly. She had a migraine all of a sudden, complete with nausea and trembling. It was like having a chasm open up at your feet. Joanna and Mike had independently shown Dominic in the worst possible light, as a cold, ruthless, untrustworthy man.

She would have dismissed it out of hand, but for the aspects which made this alternative picture of Dominic horribly credible. Dominic *was* a man far more virile than anyone she'd ever known. It was conceivable—though it conflicted with everything she knew or instinctively felt about him—that he might never be satisfied with one woman, that he might even be the satyr Joanna had described.

And if it were not true, why should anyone want to lie so cruelly about him?

'Which reminds me,' Joanna said, holding up a finger, 'have you heard ahout the latest witch-hunt on unauthorised tapping?'

'Mike Wetherall said something ...' she shrugged listlessly.

'He would do,' Joanna said meaningfully. 'He's right in the firing line, poor mug. He might end up losing his job.'

'I don't believe that,' Honor said, shaking her head. 'We've all done it.'

'Yes, but you're the head of your section,' Joanna reminded her. 'Mike's only a humble worker ant. You're entitled to know things—he's not!'

Honor stared at her. In theory, much of the magnetic information stored in the company's hardware was inaccessible. Secret user codes were needed to be able to retrieve confidential information like planning and forecasting data, and only a handful of people, like Mark MacDonald himself, or the design staff, had those codes.

In practise, the less confidential banks were quite often penetrated. In order to save time on lengthy procedures, some of the staff had found ways of bypassing the checks. Strictly speaking, tapping was against the rules, but it saved a hell of a lot of time.

And Mike, with his superior knowledge of computing, was one of the best tappers around. Honor herself and Joanna Rockley had frequently asked Mike to tap into various banks to get an urgently needed bit of 'secure' information, such as, for example, customer lists. 'Are you serious?' she asked guiltily.

'Deadly serious.' Joanna folded her arms, stretching out elegant legs. 'The trouble is that people who don't know anything about computers or computing get all sorts of stupid ideas. If the lean and hungry Mr Raven gets his claws into Mike, I don't think his job would be worth a nickel. Not in the present climate of suspicion and conspiracy. It'll be a long, long farewell to all Mike's greatness.'

'I'd speak up for him,' Honor said quietly. She'd worked with Mike Wetherall for almost five years now, and she knew perfectly well that he was no more capable of betraying Mark MacDonald than she herself was. 'If Mike gets the sack, I'll hand in my resignation,' she promised, green eyes cloudy.

But Joanna was right—people who didn't understand the business, especially people with minds as suspicious as Dominic's, could put unreasonable constructions on appearances.

'We've both egged him on to it, you know,' Joanna mused. 'I mean, we're always asking him to get stuff for us. I'd feel as guilty as hell.'

'So would I,' Honor agreed, trying to shake off the dark depression that was settling over her. 'Mike's not capable of selling secrets to the oppositon.'

'Not in a million years,' Joanna scoffed. 'He's an absolute innocent. I mean, can you imagine anyone with hair as short as Mike's betraying *anything*?'

Honor raised a smile somehow.

'You know what's at the back of all this, don't you?'

Joanna went on conspiratorially. 'There's a hush-hush new project on the go in Kent. Something big. My informants tell me that strange personages have been visiting the factory. Heard anything about it?'

'No,' Honor said flatly, refusing to be drawn into this particular line of discussion.

'Well!' Joanna ticked the points off on her fingers. 'Mr Peartree's secretary says they looked like Army officers, except they were in civvies.' She smiled thinly. 'Plus, they keep arriving in an MOD staff car. So the project's obviously a military one, right? Plus, one of the officers had a pair of wings on his tie-pin, so that means the airforce. Plus, all the research lately has been aimed at computerised training systems. Conclusion—Mark's angling for a massive new contract to supply the military with pilot-training systems.' She looked triumphant. 'And they're trying to keep it under their hats. Shows how good security really is, eh?'

'I can't stay,' Honor said shortly, turning to go. How right Dominic had been; most firms were as leaky as sieves. If poeple like Joanna only knew how dangerous lax talk could be!

'Right. Lunch at the Chinese down the street?'

'I don't think so,' Honor said. 'I'm not feeling very well.'

'If you change your mind . . .' Joanna fluttered beautifully manicured nails in farewell as Honor walked out.

In her own office, Honor sank into her chair, and rested her burning forehead on her folded arms. God, she felt awful. What Joanna had told her was going round and round her brain like some virulent poison, driving even her worries about Toby from her thoughts.

So much confusion . . . What possible reason would Mike and Joanna have to mislead her? She wanted so much to believe it was all a malicious falsehood. But she'd known them for five years—and she'd known Dominic less than five weeks. What if she was, after all, being a complete fool?

An image of those compelling eyes rose in her mind. In one important sense, at least, she'd been kidding herself about Dominic for a long time. She knew that now. She cared about him, very much indeed. She'd come to depend upon his warmth, his protection, his desire for her, the way she depended on the air she breathed.

She loved him. Enough to make this revelation a body blow from which she was still reeling.

Oh, Honor, she sighed silently, you haven't been very clever lately . . .

Was she impulsive beyond belief? It was only a few short weeks since she'd met him for the first time, and already she felt there could never be room for anyone in her heart but Dominic. Dominic, who might for all she knew be a Don Juan who cared no more for her than a child cares for a new toy.

Impulsive? But she'd had no choice about loving Dominic Raven. Love had simply come, uninvited and unwanted. Love had been thrust upon her from the start, against her will.

And when you had no choice about love, you couldn't pick and choose the qualities of the man you loved.

There was something in the female heart which drew women towards men who were wicked. She'd heard of women falling in love with the most vicious criminals—murderers, rapists, thieves. Maybe it's some mad optimism in each woman, she thought sadly, some crazy idea that *she* would be different, would reform the errant male . . .

But Honor didn't even have that illusion to excuse herself. If Dominic was the heartless seducer Joanna had described, she knew she had no chance of reforming him.

Unhappily, she remembered that conversation at Kew. *I*

wonder what love is, sometimes. He'd said those words with that dark, secret smile in his eyes. He'd talked about love and sex that day, and she'd thought he'd been teasing when he'd said that sex was more powerful than love. She'd also thought he'd been teasing when he'd told her she was naïve . . .

What *had* happened between them. Was it love? Or was it simply sex? Yet the answer was ready, even before she'd posed the question. She loved him. There was no doubt about that.

What if he didn't love her? How cruel, if so much beauty and potency were without a heart.

She picked the sheaf of sales orders out of her in-tray, and launched herself into the task of processing them. Whatever the truth was, she would discover it somehow. She would ask Dominic about Jeremy Larkin again, and get the truth this time!

She'd been working for barely an hour and a half when the call came. It was Dominic, telephoning from his office.

'Toby's trial is scheduled for Thursday,' he said briefly. 'We have to talk about him—among other things. Can you get away for lunch?'

'Yes, of course——'

'I won't have much time,' he warned her, 'because something urgent's come up, and I'm taking a train to Birmingham in a couple of hours. There's a restaurant just around the corner from Victoria Station, called Ferucci's.'

'I know it,' she nodded.

'Meet me there as close to one o'clock as you can,' Dominic commanded. 'We'll have an hour together, at any rate.'

'I will do.'

'See you at one.' With his usual lack of ceremony, he'd cut her off.

She laughed, slightly tearfully, as she put the receiver down. Was it possible the human heart could swoop between such contradictory emotions in one morning? Right now she could have hugged Dominic, covered his face with kisses, no matter what he'd done. Right now she loved him. She loved him for his strength, for the generosity with which he used it.

Ferucci's was an elegant Italian restaurant, the clay floor-tiles and roughly plastered walls evoking the Tuscan cuisine for which it was famous. It was far too expensive for her to have ever frequented it before, but the head waiter led her straight to the private corner table where Dominic was already waiting, brooding over a glass of red wine. He rose fluidly as she approached, his smile seeming to warm the whole room.

With possessive naturalness, he kissed her full on the lips, and seated her opposite him, with her back to the room. 'I want your undivided attention on me,' he said smokily, 'and not on all the flirtatious male eyes that are looking our way.'

She let him order a simple meal of *spaghetti al pomodoro* followed by grilled chicken with red peppers, and smiled at him with soft green eyes as he poured her a glass of the Chianti he'd already started on. Could what Joanna had told her really be true? Looking at him across the table, it seemed very hard to believe . . .

'We've had quite a council of war over your little brother,' he informed her, resting his chin on his interlocked fingers. 'The police have been very helpful. It turns out that last week's incident wasn't the first time Toby's been known to sell drugs. That's why he was picked up.'

'Oh, Dominic,' Honor said, her smile fading. 'I'd hoped it was just a one-off aberration.'

'Toby has some nasty friends,' Dominic said flatly. 'Very nasty. They've been taking advantage of his weakness for some time now. One of them is in custody already, and warrants are out for the arrest of two more. The danger is that there will always be others—until Toby grows up, and starts taking responsibility for his own life.'

'I don't know if he'll ever do that,' she said unhappily.

'I told Toby that there would be conditions placed on my helping him,' Dominic reminded her. The spaghetti had arrived, and Honor started curling the delicious strands around her fork. 'If your brother walks free on Thursday,' he went on, 'he'll have to fulfil his side of the bargain. And I want him out of London, Honor. It's his only chance.'

'But where could he go?' she demanded in surprise.

'I'll come straight to the point,' Dominic said quietly. 'Wavell Berkeley is a good friend of mine. He ranches a hundred thousand cattle at a place called Buchan, near Tenant Creek, in Northern Australia——'

'Australia?'

'What they call the Outback,' Dominic nodded. 'Wavell needs a handyman carpenter around the farm. The work will be unremittingly hard, and there isn't a sign of civilisation for a hundred and fifty miles in any direction. But the pay is more than adequate, and Wavell will personally vouch for Toby's good behaviour.' He smiled seriously into Honor's horror-stricken green eyes. 'Moreover, Wavell has four strapping sons and a daughter of around Toby's age who're prepared to overlook the fact that Toby's a pallid Pom, and be his friends. They know something about him already, Honor, and they're keen to help.'

'You can't be serious!' Honor said, spaghetti still dangling untasted from her frozen fork. 'You're asking Toby to leave the country and go and work as a labourer in *Australia?*'

'You don't seem to understand,' Dominic said gently. 'I'm not asking anybody's permission. Toby *is* going, Honor. His only other choice is facing up to whatever sentence the magistrate hands out.'

'But——'

'And he won't be a labourer. He'll be working with wood, putting up sheds, mending fences, making the odd bit of furniture for the farm—or whatever else Wavell tells him to do. He'll have a workshop of his own, the use of a Land Rover, and as many horses as he can get a leg over. Wavell uses a Cessna to organise the mustering, so he'll even get a chance to learn how to fly.' Dominic's handsome face was totally implacable as he spoke, and Honor's heart was sinking right into her boots. He meant it, she realised, her skin going cold. He meant every word of it. 'The boy will have a chance to settle in while Wavell sorts out a work permit and shows him round. After that, he'll be signed up for six months of hard graft at Buchan.'

'You can't possibly be serious,' she said in a breathless voice.

'I'm certainly not joking,' Dominic said coolly. 'Eat your spaghetti. It's good.' He tucked into his own plateful with relish.

'Is this your idea of helping him?' she demanded with rising anger at his calmness. 'To exile him away from his home and family, to some tiny, remote, God-forsaken corner of the globe——'

'Australia is hardly a tiny corner of the globe,' he pointed out with amusement. 'Wavell's farm is about the size of Surrey.'

'God! You think it's funny?' She put her fork down, eyes flaring green fire at him. 'It's monstrous, Dominic. This is what Mog's father did to him, and it shows the same brutal lack of humanity——'

'If it shows anything,' Dominic said silkily, 'it shows that

I care enough about your brother to give him the best chance he'll ever get in his life.' He leaned forward. 'And may I point out that the only person taking a real risk in this deal is Wavell Berkeley. I just hope Toby doesn't let him down, because I value Wavell's friendship very much. I assure you, Toby didn't make a fraction as much fuss over the idea.' Dominic smiled slightly. 'It took him a little while to get used to it, naturally.'

'But you convinced him to let himself be banished ten thousand miles away?' she supplied, her lips compressed grimly.

'Your geography is somewhat exaggerated.' Dominic had all but demolished his plate of food already, while hers lay untouched. 'But the distance itself is part of the cure. No drug-peddling cronies to lead him into trouble. No dole queue to sap his self-respect.' Wicked black eyes met hers. 'No soft-hearted sister to fall back on in every emergency.'

'Just a blistering desert,' she supplied vitriolically, 'and back-breaking work for some slave-driver of a farmer and his family of bumpkins.'

'You sound like a silly girl,' he said shortly. 'Toby's going to be happier there than he's ever been here. Wavell and his family are very far from a family of bumpkins. They're going to treat your brother with complete fairness; he'll live like one of the family, and he'll get an honest day's pay for an honest day's work, which is more than he's achieved in London.'

'You sound like a Victorian judge sending a kid to the penal colonies for stealing a—a loaf of bread.'

He arched a dark eyebrow at her. 'If you think selling cocaine is comparable to stealing a loaf of bread, you've got rocks in that beautiful head. This may sound callous, Honor,' he said quietly, 'but it really doesn't have anything to do with you. It's between me and Toby, and we're both adults. This is a good solution, believe me. The whole thing's being laid on for Toby. I'm even paying his passage there,' Dominic drank, then set the glass down. 'Now tell me,' he growled, 'what possible objection can *you* have?'

What objection? Toby—her sensitive, gentle Toby—all alone in the Outback! It was a horrible thought. He'd be miles from anywhere. Miles from the nearest doctor, miles perhaps from the nearest telephone, remote from anything she could do to help him. He was already as good as gone, in fact. With an effort, she held her anger in rein, and tried to keep her voice quiet. 'When is he supposed to be going?' she asked despairingly.

'Within a few days,' Dominic said calmly. 'He needs to get himself kitted out. His frayed jeans and trainers won't last very long at Buchan. There are various other formalities to be gone through. But the sooner he leaves the better.'

'He'll be so lonely,' she said with a catch in her voice. 'Oh, Dominic, what have you done to him?'

'Don't cry into your Chianti,' he warned mockingly, 'the salt will ruin the bouquet.'

'How can you tease me like this?' she said, the tears really threatening to spill over now.

'Because you're making a silly fuss like a silly girl,' he said gently. 'It's a great big beautiful country out there, my love. I've spent a lot of time with Wavell at Buchan, and I'm confident it'll be the making of Toby.' He leaned back, turning the glass of ruby wine in long fingers, watching her tragic expression with smiling eyes. 'They're good people, kindly and understanding. They'll do everything they can for him.'

'But they won't be his family!'

'If his family had the power to do him any good,' Dominic pointed out dispassionately, 'he wouldn't be in this fix right now. And it isn't the people that will really help him, Honor. It's the land itself. There's no room for weakness or corruption out there. The sun will burn it out of him, and the clean, dry wind will blow it away across the desert.' He smiled, teeth white and perfect against his tanned lips. 'Sure, he'll find the first few weeks hard going. But as he steadily grows hard and fit and brown, he'll learn to love it. He'll love the space, and the clean air and the way the stars blaze at night. He'll learn to rely on himself; and that will bring him a sense of perspective about himself and the world which he could never have got in this crowded grey city.'

Honor pressed her temples with her fingers giddily. Nothing would ever convince her that Dominic was right about this. 'Six months,' she said unsteadily.

'Yes,' Dominic nodded. 'He'll sign a contract for six months at Buchan. That was the condition on which the powers that be agreed to drop the charge. After those six months, he'll have the choice of coming home again, or singing on for another six months.' He nodded for the waiter to clear away Honor's untouched plate. 'It's quite possible that he'll choose to stay on. Especially,' he added with the hint of a smile, 'if Wavell's daughter has turned out the way she was promising last time I saw her.'

That did it.

Honor pushed her plate away, and stood up.

'Goodbye, Dominic.'

'Where are you going?' he asked warily.

'Away,' she said flatly. Her eyes met his, filled with pain and anger. 'I once said that you were the most destructive man I'd ever met. Then I thought you did it deliberately. Now I know that the truth is even sadder. It's something buried deep inside you, Dominic. You just can't help destroying things, can you? Destruction is your idea of tidying up the world, straightening all the ragged edges.'

He leaned back, mouth a grim line. 'Thank you for the analysis. What's your conclusion?'

'My conclusion is that you've done more harm to my family than anything since the death of my mother.' Her mouth quivered slightly. 'I thought you were going to help Toby, despite what you'd done to my sister. But never in my wildest imaginations did I dream you would come up with anything like *this*.'

'Nor did I imagine,' he replied evenly, 'that your reaction would be as juvenile and sentimental as *this*.'

'I don't want you to have anything more to do with my brother,' she said in a low, unsteady voice. 'I appreciate your efforts to help. But I'd rather he took his chances with the law, and maybe even spent some time in jail, than went through what you've got planned!'

'You were always too compassionate towards him,' Dominic retorted, black eyes growing impatient. 'Anyway, it has nothing to do with you. It's Toby's decision.'

'Then I'm going to see Toby now,' she said quietly, 'and remind him that he does have a choice, after all.'

But as she was turning to go, his fingers closed round her wrist with such biting strength that she gasped aloud.

'You're hurting me!'

'I mean to.' His eyes glittered dangerously. 'Sit down, Honor.'

She tried to pull her wrist free, but his grip was vicelike, and she only succeeded in hurting herself. 'Let me go, Dominic!'

'Not before you've heard me out. Sit.' Her eyes were hot with unshed, angry tears, but she had no option but to obey him. 'Have you ever heard the expression "killing with kindness"?' he asked grimly.

'Of course I have,' she said shortly.

'That's what you're trying to do to your brother.' He tightened his grip on her wrist as she turned away. 'You've been kind and understanding with him all his life. Too kind, to understanding. He needs something else now,

Honor—he needs firmness and control. If he doesn't get that, he'll destroy himself, and you have my personal guarantee on that. If it makes any difference to you, Helen Matthews agrees completely with my assessment.'

'Helen Matthews is in love with you,' Honor said bitterly. 'It's obvious in every look she gives you. She'd agree with you if you said day was night. And I'm getting sick of the sound of her name!'

'This isn't the time for a display of jealous spite,' he said brusquely.

'*Spite?*' she bridled. 'My family has been broken up so many times that it hardly exists any more. There are just three of us left, and we've all suffered in our various ways, believe me. And now you're trying to break us up even further!'

'Honor——'

'I wonder why?' she cut through, not finished with what she was saying. 'Shall I tell you my guess? You want me all to yourself. You've already driven a wedge between me and my sister, and now you're Macchiavellian enough to use this opportunity to send Toby out of the country.' She glared at him furiously. 'That way, there'll be no one left. I'll have no one to turn to—except *you*. Now tell me who's spiteful and jealous!'

He stared at her for a moment, taking in her quivering mouth and blazing eyes. When he at last spoke, his voice was quiet, almost sombre. 'I'm glad, at least, that you realise how much I care for you. As to the rest of what you've just said, I trust that when your temper has cooled sufficiently, you'll realise yourself what poisonous rubbish it is.'

'Then why are you doing this?' she shot back at him. 'What possible justification can you have?'

'Can't you understand?' he groaned. 'Every time Toby falls from grace, you're on hand to catch him. Every time he makes a fool of himself, you're there to forgive and forget. And every time you do those things, you weaken your brother's self-respect and self-control by a further step.' He leaned forward urgently. 'This latest venture of his is serious, Honor—really serious. If he's just forgiven and allowed to slip away this time, there may not even *be* a next time. The next time the police pick him up, he may be lying dead in an alley, with a needle stuck in his arm!'

'That's cruel,' she whispered.

'It's realistic.' He released her wrist, leaving livid marks on the fine skin. 'Please calm down,' he said more quietly. 'You're behaving like an idiot.'

'An idiot? Yes.' She chafed her wrist, aching for the strength to be able to hit back at *him*. 'An idiot for not believing the warnings my friends tried to give me.'

'What warnings?' he enquired, arching a dark eyebrow.

'About what you're really like. About your true character. About what you did to your partner, Jeremy Larkin. How you used him and then destroyed him. About how he killed himself, and you never even went to see him buried.'

'Who told you that?' She saw the colour drain away from beneath the tanned cheekbones, and knew with a further twist of the knife inside her that she'd hit home.

'It's true, isn't it?' she said grimly. 'He did kill himself, didn't he?'

'Yes,' Dominic said with an effort. 'He did kill himself.'

'Because you drove him to it!' She hit out at him again. 'Aren't you going to defend yourself? Or does it really mean that little to you?'

Now her own pain and anger was reflected in his face. 'Defend myself? No.' He bit the words out. 'If you're asking me whether I have Jeremy's death on my conscience, then the answer is also no.'

'Of course,' she sneered. 'You don't have a conscience, do you? In your line of work it's an occupational liability.'

'Stop it, Honor!' Clenching his fist, Dominic made an effort to control his emotions. It was obvious how much her accusation had shaken him, and in Honor's eyes, that was an admission of guilt which contradicted all his smooth words. 'You've been prying into areas which don't concern you,' he said tightly. 'I'd advise you to go no further.'

'The tables are turned now, aren't they?' she laughed drily. 'And the skeletons in *your* closet aren't so pretty, Dominic. Poor little Pru, at least, never harmed a living soul in her life.'

His mouth was a hard line. 'This isn't the time or place to discuss Jeremy. It isn't your right to demand it, but if you insist on knowing the truth, then let's go somewhere more private——'

'So you can have the time to invent a good cover story? No,' Honor said drily, 'I'm not that naïve, Dominic. If you've got any explanation to offer, then I want to hear it now.'

Real anger sparked in those coal-black eyes. 'You don't have any justification for talking to me like that,' he said grimly. 'Who, incidentally, is my accuser?'

'There was more than one. And they weren't connected.'

'I find *that* hard to believe,' he said with a harsh laugh. 'Honor, sometimes you're so naïve that it amazes me.'

'What amazes me,' she retorted cruelly, 'is how I ever fell for your lies!'

'If you're going,' he said tensely, 'then go now.'

She stared at him, close to tears. So much passion between them, so much love that was now immutably poisoned. 'Very well,' she said, her throat tight and painful, 'I'll go.'

She rose and walked out of the restaurant, into the busy street. The sunlight struck her like a dazzling sword, turning the tears on her eyelashes into diamonds. She walked blindly to the pedestrian crossing, her heart feeling as though it would break.

She heard a shout behind her, and too late, tried to step back on to the kerb.

At the edge of her vision, the bus loomed gigantic and red, its brakes squealing in anguish as the frantic driver tried vainly to avoid her.

The impact was huge, numbing. She felt herself flung across the street like a doll, felt her body hit the iron railings and crumple to the pavement, but there was no pain. Only noise and confusion.

She lay staring up at the sky, green eyes wide open, her raven hair tumbled across her face, and could feel no movement in her body.

There were people crowding round, their faces expressing shock. She heard a woman's voice gasp, 'She's dead!', and someone else warn, 'Don't move her, don't touch her.'

Then Dominic was with her, strong arms lifting her slender body out of the road with infinite care. Dazedly, she looked up into his pale face, and tried to smile.

'Hello,' she whispered. 'Not looking where I'm going, as usual.'

'It weren't my fault! She just stepped right out in front of me.' The bus driver, white with shock, peered over Dominic's shoulder, then grimaced in horror. 'Oh, bleedin' hell!'

'Not your fault.' Her eyes sought Dominic's, wanting to tell him how sorry she was. 'Am I badly hurt?' she heard herself ask.

'Yes,' he said tightly, stroking her cheek. 'Now lie still until the ambulance arrives.'

'I can't move,' she whimpered.

'It's all right,' he soothed, as though talking to a child. She knew that gentleness of his so well, loved it so much. There was blood on his hand now, red and messy. Her blood. 'Why did I let you go?' he muttered savagely to himself.

'Don't let me walk out on you again,' she said with a little laugh. 'It's not safe away from you.'

'You're never going anywhere without me again,' he said quietly. 'I'm not going to let you out of my sight again.' His eyes narrowed as he explored her injuries with feather-light fingertips. 'Can you feel that?'

'I can't feel anything.'

Something was happening inside her head, as though the whole universe were tilting steadily upside down. 'Dominic!' she called in terror, but there was no reply. Only the darkness that rushed up to swallow her.

CHAPTER NINE

PERIODS of consciousness were brief pools of light in a dark, dark sea. Honor was aware mainly of raging pain.

Also of waking at odd hours and seeing strangers, of being wheeled down corridors on a trolley. Then of immobility, her body and limbs held in a huge clamp of unbearable tightness.

A long nightmare, in which confused visions of Dominic haunted her, in which she whimpered with pain and loneliness.

Then, one morning, the curtains were pulled open by a smiling student nurse, and sunlight filled the little room. Honor struggled with sleep, opening cracked lips to plead for water. No sound came out, but the nurse had guessed what she wanted.

'Doctor will be pleased,' she said brightly, holding the cup gently to Honor's mouth. 'Now you'll be able to admire his handiwork properly.'

She lay back against the pillow, exhausted, and felt the sick ache start to flood her senses. 'God, I feel awful,' she whispered.

'Not surprising.'

'How long have I been here?'

'You were admitted six days ago,' the nurse told her. She had bright blue eyes and wispy blonde hair peeping from under her white cap.

'Six days!' Honor stared around the room blankly, unable to grasp it fully. Masses of flowers, a window that let in a great square of blue sky, the sanitised neatness of a hospsital room.

'You're private,' the little nurse smiled, 'that's why you've got a ward all to yourself.'

Six days out of her life, lost for ever. 'What happened to me?' she asked numbly. With a flash of horror she remembered her inability to move as she'd lain in Dominic's arms. 'Am I paralysed?'

'You're covered in plaster.' The nurse tapped Honor's shoulder gently, her nail clicking on the plaster of Paris. 'That's why you can't move. But all your reflexes are OK.'

'My reflexes . . . How badly was I hurt?'

'Five broken ribs,' the nurse said promptly, 'fractured right clavicle, fractured right humerus, compound fracture of the right hand, thirty-eight stitches in various places, and quite severe concussion.' She straightened Honor's coverlet with relish. 'Dr Austen himself did the fixations, which shows how interesting you were. You've got more steel rivets in you than Metal Mickey.'

'Dominic,' she said, closing her eyes at the catalogue of pain. 'Dominic Raven—a tall, dark man—has he been here?'

'Hmmm,' the nurse said with a dreamy smile. 'I know just the one you mean.'

'Is—is he here?'

'He's been here every night,' the nurse sighed, her expression appreciative. 'Pity. If you'd woken two hours ago, you'd have seen him.' Enviously, she folded her slim arms. 'He seems to think an awful lot of you—he's dead worried about you.'

'Can you get a message to him?' she asked, her voice dry and papery. Her abiding memory was of the cruel things she'd said to Dominic just before the accident, and her need to apologise to him burned in her, alongside her physical pain. When she'd hurt herself, she'd also hurt him—and while she'd been unconscious Dominic would have been going through hell. 'Please?'

'I'm going to ring him now,' the blonde nurse soothed. 'He left strict instructions that he was to be kept informed about you. He'll be here soon enough,' she smiled. 'You just worry about getting yourself better. You've been through a very nasty trauma.' She got up briskly. 'I'll try and bring you a cup of tea before the doctor arrives.'

Honor turned her head fretfully on the pillow as the nurse left. Her whole body was a mass of pain. With a shaky left hand, she traced the contours of her right side. Her entire right arm and shoulder were encased in a rigid plaster cast. Another tight bandage hugged her ribs, just under her breasts. There were more bandages in other places.

Oddly, it occurred to her to remember that she hadn't been back to work since that lunch with Dominic. It was a weird sensation, of taking up her conscious self again. Like taking up a life again. Sorting through her confused mind for the loose ends and unresolved connections she'd left behind six days ago . . .

Toby. It suddenly occurred to her that she'd been lying unconscious right through Toby's trial. A sudden frantic anxiety was gradually replaced by painful resignation. Whatever had happened to him, there wasn't anything she could do here and now. And she knew that Dominic would have done his utmost to protect Toby, despite all the cruel things she'd said to him that day . . .

When the little blonde nurse returned, she was preceded by a middle-aged doctor in a yellow bow-tie.

'I've had my own grievances against London Transport from time to time,' he said as he peered into her eyes through an instrument, 'but I've never chosen to argue with them in quite such a personal fashion. Welcome to St Robert's, Miss O'Hara. You'll be pleased to know that the bus wasn't too badly damaged.'

She tried to raise a smile, but it wasn't a very bright one.

She was growing more awake and aware by the minute now. 'Can my family be told that I'm awake?' she pleaded. 'I really want to speak to them.'

'Your sister's here right now,' the doctor nodded. 'She's in the waiting-room, and very relieved that you're awake. You can speak to her just as soon as I've examined you.' He smiled gently. 'You'd also better know exactly what Dr Austen has done to your arm.' He lifted a large X-ray photograph from the folder at the foot of her bed. 'The fractures to your upper arm and shoulder were quite severe, as you can see. A number of steel pins have been inserted to hold the bones rigid while they heal.'

Honor stared silently at the black rods, clearly visible through the ghostly grey image of the bone, and remembered that terrible, numbing blow as the doctor explained the complex surgery she'd been through.

'The human body is a fragile organism,' the doctor nodded, watching her dawning comprehension of how narrowly she'd escaped disability or death. 'Now, stop worrying about anyone or anything else. Nurse Edwards, will you help me to lift her slightly, please?'

The examination lasted ten minutes. Honor's pain was increasing steadily, and when the doctor left, warning her that she was scheduled for another X-ray that afternoon, the nurse gave her two pain-killers and a glass of water.

She lay in the quiet, bright room, waiting for the ache to fade away. It was going to be at least three weeks before the plaster came off, and for a long time after that she was going to have to wear a sling. A long time away from work, a lot of discomfort and boredom. She turned her head to look at the flowers at her bedside. There were masses of them; huge clouds of red roses, sprays of white and yellow lilies, a posy of honeysuckle which she recognised as having come from her own garden.

There were cards, too. With her good hand, she fumbled

for them, and read the loving messages. From Mark MacDonald, Mike Wetherall, Toby, Prudence, the girls at work, friends and relations across the country. And one from Dominic. The message was simply *Get well.* A command? A plea?

A rustle at the door heralded Prudence. Honor smiled a tired welcome, but Pru had burst into tears.

'You're awake,' she sobbed. 'Thank God. I've been so worried about you!' She hurried up to the bed, and took Honor's good hand in both her own. 'You've been lying here like—like a waxwork.' She went on tearfully. 'So pale and calm and beautiful—as if—as if you were d-dead!'

'I'm alive, if not kicking,' Honor said tenderly, shaking Pru's hands gently. 'I'm sorry if I frightened you.'

'We've all been terrified.' Pru wiped her eyes. 'You've been through about six operations——'

'Tell me about Toby,' Honor interrupted, laying a hand on her sister's mouth. 'What happened in court?'

'Oh, Toby's landed on his feet, as usual,' Pru said with a shaky smile. She looked at Honor with an odd expression in her reddened eyes. 'So many things have happened while you've been in hospital, love. It's all going to be rather a shock for you.'

'Tell me,' Honor commanded in dread.

'I'm not sure if you're really strong enough,' Pru hesitated.

'What's happened to Toby?' she repeated tightly.

'He got off,' Pru told her. 'Or rather, Dominic and that slinky friend of his got him off. The magistrate said he was more a victim than anything else. Anyway, the poor victim's getting ready to go to Australia, the lucky dog. He's as excited as a kid.'

'Is he?' Honor stared out of the window in silence. Perhaps her mind had been working on the idea while she'd been unconscious, because now she felt with inner certainty that Dominic was right. That his offer to Toby had been incredibly generous and wise, and that her own spiteful reaction had been ill-judged and childish. 'When does he go?'

'In ten days' time,' Pru said. 'He's so happy. He really thinks this is a chance for him to get his life together. He's absolutely delighted . . . He thinks Dominic's the bee's knees, of course.' She nodded at the mass of fragrant red roses at Honor's bedside. 'Those are from Dominic.'

'I guessed,' Honor smiled wearily. The pain was starting to seep out of her bones, but it was still there, throbbing in tune with her heart. 'The nurse said he'd been here every night.'

'Almost all of the time,' Pru nodded. 'He just sits beside you, watching you. He cares a great deal for you, you know.'

'Yes, I think he does.' She touched Pru's cheek. 'And I think I care a great deal for him, Pru. How do you feel about that?'

'I'm glad for you,' Pru said simply. Her cheeks were suddenly flushed and hot. 'He's a good man, Honor. And I've been incredibly stupid.'

'What about?' Honor asked affectionately.

'About everything.' She looked up at her sister, the colour right in her cheeks. 'It's all such a tangle.'

'Pru . . .' She took Prudence's hand. 'What's this all about?'

'It's about Dominic Raven,' Pru said with a sigh. 'And me.'

'Go on,' Honor said quietly.

'I told you I'd met him a few times, before Mog went to America,' Pru said, 'and that I liked him. Well, I liked him rather too much.' She twisted her hands into a knot, her soft skin still scarlet under Honor's incredulous gaze. 'It all sounds so crazy and humiliating, but I think I've aged five years since then. He was so interested in me, you see. He always took time out to talk to me. I got into the way of flirting with him, just being a fool.' Pru's hazel eyes met Honor's briefly. 'You know better than I do what an attractive man he is. He can make you feel like the only girl in the world when he looks at you like that. I guess—I guess it was a kind of insane vanity, but I thought he was fancying me. It wasn't that I'd stopped caring for Mog—I just thought I could get away with it. He went to my head, Honor, like something you've drunk that's far stronger than you're used to!'

'What happened?' Honor asked tightly.

'I tried to get him to go to bed with me,' Pru said miserably.

'Oh, Pru!' Honor sagged back. The emotions inside her were a twisted skein of unhappiness—anger, sorrow, sudden bitter understanding. 'Is *that* why he told Mog's father the marriage would be unwise?'

'It must have been. Yes, yes, it was.' Her face as pale now as it had been red before, Pru touched Honor's shoulder. 'This is a genuinely horrible shock for you, isn't it?'

'It is rather,' Honor said in a constricted voice. The pain was pounding along her bones now, and she felt awful, but she wanted to hear this through to the end.

'I won't go into any details of what I did,' Pru said dismally. 'It was too embarrassingly pathetic, and my only excuse is that I was very tipsy at the time. But I made it very clear I was available—and he turned me down flat.' She gulped. 'And it'll take me the rest of my life to forget the look on his face.'

Honor closed her eyes and lay back against the pillows. With a flash of further pain, she realised in exactly what contempt Dominic must have been holding her family all this while. A drunken father, a brother in jail, a sister without morals. 'You little idiot,' she said quietly, opening her eyes slowly. 'And all this sanctimonious talk about the way Dominic had betrayed you——'

'I was so frightened that he'd tell you,' Pru said tearfully. 'I didn't have the courage to tell you myself. But when it was obvious that you and he were sweet on each other, I was just waiting in dread for him to tell you . . .'

'Does Mog know what happened?' Honor asked sharply.

'His father told him,' Pru nodded with a tragic expression. 'That was really why he went to America. I knew the whole time that it was all my fault, but I didn't know how to tell you. Dominic must have come to the conclusion that I was a little tramp——'

'Yes,' Honor gritted, 'that's a fair conclusion.'

'—and when Morgan Lambert asked for his opinion, he must have said something. And Mog's father must have told him——' Pru winced. 'I think it almost broke Mog's heart.'

'Oh, Pru . . .'

'I felt so awful about it, and there was nothing I could do or say. I didn't even know his address. But he wrote to me from New York about three weeks ago, thank God. I was about ready to jump into the Thames by then. I wrote back, explaining everything, and telling him how much I really loved him, that it had been a terrible mistake.'

Honor stared at her sister in silence, not knowing what to say. So much she hadn't known, so much that would have helped her understand. So much that would have made her own relationship with Dominic that much simpler and clearer. 'And Mog forgave you?' Honor asked drily, thinking of the letters.

'We love each other,' Pru said, wiping the fresh tears off her lids again. 'Please believe me, Honor. Nothing's changed between us . . .'

'Of course things have changed,' Honor reminded her acidly. 'Mog's in New York, that's what's changed.' She paused. 'Or are you and Mog planning some kind of elopement together?'

'That's something else you don't know,' Pru said hesitantly. 'Mog's back in London. We're seeing each other again.'

'You're joking!'

'No.' For the first time, Pru's full mouth curved into a trembly smile. 'It's all come true, Honor. He got back while you were in here. And Mog's father isn't going to stop him from seeing me any more. He's been absolutely marvellous. You know, he was only acting to protect his son, not out of vindictiveness . . .'

'You mean the wedding is still on?' Honor demanded incredulously.

Pru shook her head earnestly. 'No—but that's not because anyone's stopping us. We love each other, Honor—but we've both realised that we might not be ready for marriage yet. We had a long talk two nights ago, all of us—including Dominic—and we've agreed that we'll wait for a year or so, and just be together. Then, if we really want to, we'll get married. But not until we're both absolutely sure of each other—and ourselves.'

Honor laughed softly, her anger ebbing away in the delight of it. 'How on earth did all this come about?' she asked.

'Dominic,' Pru said simply. 'He persuaded Mog's father to let him come home. He's extraordinary, Honor. He seems to understand everything about you, without your even having to speak. I've been absolutely open with him. I've admitted that I made a terrible mistake, but he knows I've never stopped loving Mog!'

'You've been very lucky, piglet.'

'I used to think that I'd die if you ever took up with Dominic Raven,' Pru said seriously. 'But now I pray it happens. You're so perfectly suited to each other, both so calm and wise . . .'

Dominic. Honor watched the white clouds drift across the heavenly blue of the sky. That tall, potent figure stood at so many points of her life now. His wisdom and his protection drawing her into safety, offering her help, comfort, love.

'You're tired,' Pru said guiltily, getting up. 'I knew this was all going to be too much for you. I'll let you sleep now.'

'Stay,' Honor whispered. 'There's so much I want to know . . .'

'Later,' Pru promised, kissing her forehead lightly. 'Your Dominic will be here soon. He'll tell you everything. Just sleep now.'

When Pru had gone, Honor lay between waking and sleep, her eyes closed. What Prudence had just told her was drifting round inside her head. Of course Dominic would think Pru shallow and unworthy! She thought hotly of the way she'd defended Pru to Dominic, abusing him with ignorant cruelty. And all the time, he'd known far better than she herself had how much Pru deserved censure. She ought to have known that his judgement couldn't have been so far wrong . . .

Yet he'd never betrayed Pru's embarrassing secret to Honor. She felt a warm sense of appreciation healing her shame. At least he'd spared her that humiliation.

But despite her new knowledge of Pru's folly, Honor also felt instinctively that Pru was genuinely contrite—and that her relationship with Mog would grow more strongly and truly than ever before. Her brief flare of anger at Pru had long since faded into pity by now. She knew enough about her sister to know that she'd learned a very bitter lesson, and that this miraculous second chance would not be wasted.

So perfectly suited? Sleep overwhelmed her, dark and

warm as a man's eyes.

When she next opened her eyes, it was twilight. She'd slept the whole day away. Her dreams had been of Dominic, dreams that were potent and sweet and fulfilling. A deep peace filled her as she lay in the soft light, long lashes veiling her eyes sleepily.

But when she felt the warm touch on her cheek, she knew intuitively who it was.

'Dominic!'

'I was beginning to wonder when I'd ever see those wonderful green eyes open again,' he said huskily.

'Sorry to keep you waiting.' She rubbed her cheek against his hand, like an adoring cat, and raised her eyes to his dark figure, seated beside her. 'Have you been here long?'

'Since this morning,' he smiled. 'You've hardly stirred all day. But for the first time in a week, there was some colour in your cheeks. You looked very different. And you were smiling. What were you dreaming of?'

'You don't have to be told. Do you?'

He leaned forward, and kissed her on the lips, the caress of his mouth warm and intoxicatingly sweet. 'I've missed you,' he whispered. 'Don't ever do that to me again.'

'I never will.' She touched his face. 'I don't ever want to be away from your side.'

'That's easily arranged,' he replied softly. 'How do you feel?'

'In heaven—now.'

'I meant your shoulder,' he pointed out gravely.

'It hurts,' she admitted, 'but it's a very effective reminder of my own stupidity. I've always thought myself very clever, Dominic, but today I've realised just how stupid and blind I've really been.'

'Hush,' he said gently.

'I won't hush. I want to talk to you. Pru was here this morning,' she told him, lacing her fingers through his.

'Yes,' he nodded. 'I know. I spoke to her earlier.'

'My family seems to have been taking up a great deal of your time lately,' Honor sighed. She struggled to find the words. 'Prudence told me about what happened between you and her, before—before Mog went to America.'

'Is that really important now?' he enquired, and she could hear the smile in his voice.

'It is to me! I didn't know about that, Dominic. I didn't have the faintest idea that anything of the sort had happened, or I wouldn't have been so hostile towards you from the start.' Honor groaned, the plaster cast cutting into her soft skin. 'I'm not putting this very well at all! But I feel so ashamed of Pru, and ashamed of myself for defending her so fiercely, when all the time . . .'

'Of course you had no idea. But like Toby's folly, it's hardly a matter for you to feel shame over.'

'OK, then call it concern,' she amended. 'But I realise how you came to your conclusion about Prudence, now. It's natural you would think her shallow and immoral after what she did. I can still hardly believe it myself.'

'I told you once before,' he reminded her drily, 'that the emotions of nineteen are often unpredictable. I don't think that Pru's immoral. I've grown to like her a good deal—especially now that I've seen how much your accident upset her.' He touched her lips with his fingertips. 'It used to anger me that she and Toby took you so much for granted, my love. They simply accepted your goodness and kindness, your abundant love, as if it was their right. They gave so little in return. It was one of the things that most showed how much they needed to learn, both of them.'

'They love me in their way,' she smiled.

'They'll learn to love you more,' he said softly. 'Almost losing you has been a revelation to your family, green eyes.

I think they're just beginning to understand what yo
to them.'

'I trust them to always love me, just because of who I am,'
she said gently. 'It's you I care about, Dominic. A long time ago I said some horrible things to you——'

'My ways are too rough,' he said flatly. 'Whatever you said to me that day was richly deserved.' He sighed. 'I was mad to break the idea to you so flippantly, and then to come on so heavy. I'd never have sent Toby to Australia without your approval of the scheme. I just wasn't prepared for your resistance, so I tried to bully you into agreement——'

'The idea is a wonderful one,' she stopped him from apologising further. 'And from what I hear, the rest of the family, including Toby, think so too.' She stroked his hand. 'What I meant was that I know it isn't true that you're destructive. You're anything but destructive. And those accusations I made; they were false, and I know that in my heart. I just used them as weapons.'

'They mean very little.' Dominic leaned back in his chair, his voice gentle. 'But I have to give you an explanation.' He passed her a glass of water, and she sipped gratefully at the cold fluid. 'I didn't destroy Jeremy Larkin,' he said painfully. 'But I watched him destroy himself. He was a brilliant electronics engineer, and we worked on a lot of projects together about fifteen years ago. A lot of his ideas are still embodied in Raven Security equipment. I was very fond of him, Honor. He was very young, much younger than I was, and a pathetic, lovable person, with an intellect that far outstripped his emotional maturity. We made a fair bit of money together in those early days; but where I was intent on building up Raven Security, Jeremy was hunting and being hunted by his own personal devils. They were mainly drugs and alcohol, but gambling and sex came into it, too.'

He was silent for a while. Honor could sense the grief in

him, and she said nothing, just held his hand and waited for him to go on.

'He ran out of money in the end, because what we were making wasn't enough for the life-style he was trying to lead. He had a small share in Raven Security, which he sold to me. But as he destroyed his mind with whisky and heroin, the brilliant ideas stopped coming. There was nothing left in his brain except hunger for the things that were destroying him. So he started begging from me. At first I helped him as much as I could, tried to get him to see doctors, go into hospitals—but he simply used the money I gave him to destroy himself still further. So I stopped giving him money.' Dominic laughed painfully. 'He was no longer the same person—he was a burned-out parody of himself. He turned against me with crazy bitterness, telling everyone I'd robbed him, calling me his exploiter. People who knew Jeremy understood that it meant nothing. But people who didn't tended to believe him—and so for a while the story spread. It hurt, of course, but there wasn't much I could do about it.'

'I'm sorry, Dominic,' she murmured.

'It was Jeremy who needed pity, not me.' He patted her hand with a smile. 'Anyhow, it's all a long, long way in the past. It's been at least a decade since anyone mentioned Jeremy's name to me, which is why it was rather a shock to hear it coming from your lips.'

'Oh, love,' she said remorsefully, 'I wish I'd never opened my mouth——'

'Don't be silly,' Dominic said, hushing her. 'Mike Wetherall has a long memory for grievances—his own or other peoples'.'

'But why?' she asked restlessly. 'Why would they tell me such horrible things about you?'

'Don't you know?' he replied gently. 'Not even now?'

It was dark in the room by now, but the sorrow in

Honor's heart was even darker. 'Yes,' she said heavily, 'I do know. I knew it as soon as Joanna repeated the same poisonous farrago that Mike had already told me. I just couldn't believe it, Dominic. I've worked side by side with them for more than four years!'

'Very few things are clear-cut in this life, my darling.' He kissed her sorrowful mouth tenderly. 'Least of all treachery. In their way, I suppose Mike and Joanna could have been as loyal to ComTech as you or anyone else. A combination of opportunity, conspiracy, and fallible human emotion turned them around.'

'Then it was Mike who sold out the LP-550?' she said in a small voice, like a child hoping to be reassured that there was nothing, after all, under the bed.

'Yes,' he said quietly. 'With a little help and a lot of encouragement, possibly sexual, from Joanna Rockley.'

Honor felt sick. 'How did you find out?'

'Mark and I had suspected for some time. The information came from various sources. The factory in Kent was one; various people there knew that Mike Wetherall took a keen interest in the development of new designs, but no one suspected that he would ever sell the information he got into the habit of scrounging.' He smiled grimly. 'As I said, most firms are as leaky as sieves. Confirmation came from outside ComTech—from the companies who bought the information about the LP-550. You see, when Mike had put together as much of the plans as he could—partly by tapping directly into the ComTech design banks—he and Joanna sold them to a middleman, who subsequently took them to other firms as original research.' He smiled drily. 'Trouble was, the middleman was too clever—he sold them to not one, but two other companies. There was general fury when no less than three revolutionary new microprocessors came on the market last autumn. It wasn't too difficult to trace the trail back to Mike.'

'Oh, Dominic,' Honor said tiredly, 'how awful. I never dreamed . . .'

'Of course not. You're too innocent.'

He switched on the bedside lamp. In the warm light, the male beauty of his face leaped out at her, catching her heart and robbing her of breath. He was so magnificent, this man of hers . . .

'That's why they were so hostile to my presence at ComTech,' he smiled, unaware of her silent worship of him. 'And so eager to blacken my name to you, too. They felt that our closeness was a threat to them.'

She thought of Mike's kindness, his sad sense of humour. 'It's almost impossible to believe,' she sighed.

'Joanna's motivation was pure greed. Mike's reasons are deeper and more complex. A general disillusionment with life is probably the main cause. But seeing you promoted over his head probably tilted the scales that final extra inch.'

'I thought he really liked me,' she said unhappily.

'He does,' Dominic smiled. 'Everyone likes you, green eyes. It's himself he hates.'

'What's going to happen to them?' she asked sadly.

'They clearly can't go on working at ComTech,' he said decisively. 'I've spoken to them both this week, and there's no question that they're guilty. It's up to Mark MacDonald, of course, but I doubt there'll be any legal action. By my guess they'll both quietly resign at once, and neither of them will ever work in computing again.' He paused. 'Mike Wetherall had the grace to regret the things he said to you about me. He was genuinely shocked by the accident, and I think he rather blamed himself for what had happened. Anyway, he wanted to send you his apology.'

Honor drew a deep breath, then reached out her hand to

Dominic. 'It's all over, isn't it?' she said softly. 'There are no more barriers between us.'

'No more barriers,' he nodded. In the darkness she caught the glint of his smile. 'I wonder whether we'll be able to stand each other without some cause of friction to liven up the proceedings?'

'I'll be able to stand you for as long as I live,' she smiled. 'Or as long as you want me.'

'Do you mean that?' He laughed quietly. 'I've sometimes wondered whether you really know how much I care for you, Honor. My need for you isn't a temporary thing. It goes very deep, my beloved, and it has no ending.'

'Are you asking me to marry you?' she asked innocently.

'You know damned well I am,' he growled.

Honor twined her good arm round his neck, staring up at his face with adoring eyes. 'My God,' she whispered, almost too full to speak. 'I love you so very much, Dominic.'

His eyes narrowed smokily as his hand touched her cheek, brushing her full mouth. 'Honor.' His voice was low and husky as he whispered her name. 'If you knew what those words mean to me ...'

'I'd have said them ages ago if I hadn't been so arrogant and stupid,' she whispered.

'Then say them again,' he commanded, his voice a husky growl.

She did, lifting her lips to his, yielding to the mastery of his kiss, shuddering at the sweet invasion he was inflicting on her mouth. His power and passion overwhelmed her, exalted her. This was how it would always be. This ecstasy was only a tiny fragment of the ocean of love that lay in store for them.

'At least you managed to keep your left hand out of plaster,' Dominic said gently, taking something out of his pocket. 'That suggests presence of mind, my love.'

She fumbled the neat leather box open single-handed.

The exquisite diamond, flawless as her happiness, blazed in the lamplight. Her hand was shaking helplessly as he took it from her, and slid it over her finger. 'I've wanted you from the minute I saw you,' he said quietly, looking into her eyes. 'First it was simply desire. You're my ideal of perfection in a woman, Honor. Slender, graceful, with those dazzling green eyes and that silky hair——' He smiled, touching her lips. 'But there was much, much more to come. I hardly knew that I was falling in love with you, day by day, hour by hour. There was so much to find out about you—like your gentleness, your intelligence, your spirit . . . You got into my blood, like a fever. I'm not an angel, my love, and it's been very hard for me to hold back sometimes . . .'

'You'll never have to hold back again,' she promised huskily. 'I've never wanted a man the way I want you!'

'I love you,' he said simply. 'And I need you, all of you, for ever!'

'Will I be enough for you?' she asked quietly. 'Won't you get bored with me?'

'Once upon a time,' he smiled, 'I couldn't bring myself to admit that I could be so moved by a single woman, could be made to burn with passion, to long for a touch from someone's lips, or a glance from someone's eyes. Total commitment had always eluded me, frightened me, even. But with you it just comes naturally. And that's the way I'll always be, Honor. Yours.'

'Even though I'm rather naïve about men?' she teased.

'This damned plaster,' he whispered. 'Just wait until it comes off.' He knelt at her bedside, taking her gently in his arms. She pressed her face against his shoulder, her heart pounding against her bruised ribs, more blissfully happy than she could ever have dreamed. 'I've fought you so long,' she mumbled gently. 'but you're so very easy to love . . .'

'As long as I stay that way to you, my sweet green eyes,' he said, his mouth brushing her eyelids shut.

'Pru's right,' she whispered. 'You're so very wise.' Honor smiled, tracing the line of his face with her fingers. 'How come you're so clever?'

'No, Honor. I'm just very, very lucky. And sometimes I can be very stupid, believe me. It was insanity that let me sit there and watch you walk out of Ferucci's. When I heard the scream of the brakes, my heart stopped inside me. I knew that if you were dead, my own life would be over for ever.'

'I'm not that easy to get rid of,' she laughed contentedly, her eyes soft.

'Nor am I.' He brushed her lips with his own. She looked up into his midnight-dark eyes, losing herself in their potent depths. 'I won't ever forget the sight of you lying in that road, so still and motionless . . . I've never known a woman like you, Honor. The day you become my wife will be the happiest day I've ever lived through.'

'Don't say any more, just yet,' she pleaded. 'So much has happened just lately that I'm afraid this is just a dream, and that any puff or breeze will blow you away from me . . .'

He touched her mouth with his fingertips. 'We're getting married next month, green eyes.'

'Is that an order?' she murmured. 'Or do I have any say in the matter?'

'None whatsoever.'

'Ah, well, you already have my soul,' she told him. 'Why not take the rest of me?'

'That's an offer,' he said, kissing her parted lips, his eyes promising passion that would shake her to the core, 'that I can't refuse.'

The sun blazed down from a sky deeper and bluer than any English sky could ever be. It baked down on the field where the slim woman in jeans and a lightweight cotton shirt was cantering a glossy black pony.

Her wide-brimmed hat had blown off, and was held on only by the ribbon tied round her slender throat. Despite the fact that her right arm was in a sling, she was riding well and gracefully, the beautiful contours of her body moving in perfect rhythm with the horse.

She urged the animal into a final gallop across the paddock, and then reined him up beside the little group of people who were sitting on the railings, watching her.

'Beaut,' Wavell Berkeley said flatly. Which was as high praise as he ever gave anyone for anything.

Laughing and panting, Honor slid off the saddle into her man's strong arms. He kissed her hard and quickly. 'Well done,' Dominic said softly.

'My go!'

Dominic slipped an arm round her waist as they watched Toby jump up into the saddle.

A tanned, fit, happy Toby, whose bright green eyes were full of a life and enthusiasm she hadn't seen in them since her childhood. With a confidence she could never hope to match, he raced off on the black pony, his hair streaming in the wind.

'Wish that brother of yours would cut his damned hair,' Wavell complained; but the note in his voice was affectionate. 'He looks like a bloody girl.'

'It suits him, Dad.' Shona Berkeley, radiant with the healthy beauty of twenty, watched Toby with speculative eyes. 'He's got the measure of that pony, at any rate. He'll make the Creek polo team this summer.'

'He's a changed boy,' Wavell nodded. 'Three months at Buchan have done wonders for him.'

'I hope he's being useful to you, Wavell,' Honor said, watching Toby.

'Hardest little grafter I ever saw,' Wavell grinned. 'I thought he was supposed to be a problem kid!'

'He's no problem,' Shona said smoothly.

'Still a bit skinny,' Wavell mused.

'Lean, Dad.' Shona's eyes followed Toby. 'You should have seen the girls crowd round him at the dance on Saturday.'

'Polo, long hair, dancing,' rumbled Wavell. 'You'd think nobody had any work to do around here.'

'Some of us are on holiday, anyway,' Dominic smiled. 'Stop complaining about anything—you've got a little slice of heaven here, haven't you?'

'Never said I didn't,' Wavell grinned.

'Is he going to be all right?' Honor asked Dominic.

'He's all right already.' He took a last look at Toby's figure, then walked Honor slowly down the field, to the clump of massive bluegums that broke the magnificent distant vista of violet hills and golden plains.

'God,' she said, leaning against his hard body, 'I'm so very happy. Do you think it's healthy to be this happy?'

'No question.' He bent to kiss her hard on the lips. She closed her eyes helplessly, touching his cheek with her fingers. 'What about your career?' he murmured. 'When we get back to England, won't you miss ComTech, and your job?'

'Mike and Joanna poisoned it for me,' she said, shaking her glossy head. 'But I wouldn't have wanted to work anyway, Dominic. I want to make you a good wife.' Her voice softened. 'And make a good mother to our children.'

He laid his hand gently on her stomach, and smiled into her eyes. 'That's a hopelessly unliberated ambition, my darling.'

'No. It's a hopefully liberated one,' she laughed. 'Being happy, and making you happy, are all the goals I'll ever want. And you?' she whispered. 'Are you happy?'

'In every fibre of my being.'

They wandered in the cool, scented shade of the gum trees. Honor's throat was almost hoarse from talking, planning, laughing—she hadn't felt so alive, so happy, in her life. The inner radiance she felt seemed to have flooded her whole spirit, giving her a new kind of beauty, a beauty that made Dominic watch her with that infathomable smile on his lips, his eyes exulting in her joy.

There was suddenly so much to do, a whole life to map out with Dominic. Her world seemed to have been purged of sorrows. Pru and Toby were happier and more mature than she'd ever seen them, and new life was growing fast within her own body.

She thought quietly of the course of their love, from that stormy first meeting at ComTech, through to the glorious white wedding that had taken place barely two months ago. 'I'll never forget the first time you kissed me.' The look she sent him from under long lashes was as provocative an invitation as ever a woman gave a man. Hidden among the sighing trees, he took her in his arms, making her heart pound as though it were going to burst.

'You don't know what you *do* to me!' she gasped, minutes later, staring up at him with drowning eyes.

'I only have to look into my own heart,' he said huskily. 'Then I know everything.' His fingers trailed across the golden column of her throat, then caressed downwards to her breasts. Honor felt her senses swim as his fingers trailed over the soft swell of her woman's body, cupping her breast with desirous possession.

'I like it best when you don't wear a bra,' he smiled.

'I'll get too big,' she warned. 'Especially in a few months' time.'

'I think you got pregnant to trap me into marrying you,' he said huskily, eyes brooding hungrily on her mouth.

'That's not true, Dominic Raven.' Her eyes sparkled green fire at him. 'You didn't know I was pregnant when you married me!'

'Didn't I?' He kissed her mouth. 'Ah well, perhaps I

didn't. But you did.'

'I had to give my child a name.' She snuggled into his arms. 'I'll never forget your expression when I told you!'

'You were supposed to be taking care of—that sort of thing,' he grinned. 'Deceiver!'

'You mean you aren't glad?' she asked innocently.,

'No,' he replied calmly, 'I'm not glad. *Glad* doesn't even begin to describe it. Overwhelmed, maybe, delighted, enraptured, awestruck ...'

'We won't make any mistakes with our children, will we?' she asked him.

'No.' He lay down on the grass, and pulled her down beside him. 'We won't make any mistakes.' She lay on her back, raven hair tumbled out, and looked up into his magnificent face. 'Happiness has to be worked at, green eyes.' His kiss was so intoxicating that she barely noticed the tanned fingers that expertly unfastened the pearl buttons of her shirt.

'Hey,' she whispered. 'What if someone comes?'

'Nobody follows newlyweds into the woods,' he murmured, kissing her naked throat with warm, hungry lips. 'Besides, it's time we worked on a little more happiness. Don't you think?'